Hello, friends of Katie Kazoo!

People often ask me why I write for kids. The answer is simple: I love kids. I think they're the most interesting people there are. When *I* was a kid, I loved reading all kinds of books—especially funny ones. So that's what I write. Funny books that will hopefully help kids learn to love to read as much as I do.

The idea for the Katie Kazoo, Switcheroo series actually came to me while I was sleeping. I had a dream about a girl who turned into a hamster. When I woke up, I knew I had to write about that girl. Today, Katie has been on more than forty switcheroo adventures, but they all started with that one crazy dream.

I can't tell you how much fun it is to write the Katie Kazoo, Switcheroo books. Sometimes when I'm writing, I laugh out loud—which makes my dog think I'm actually going a little nuts. I hope the stories in this book make you laugh just as hard.

May all *your* wishes come true—one, two . . . SWITCHEROO!

xo,

Nancy Krulik

Katie Kazoo
SWITCHEROO

A Collection of Katie
Books 1-4

Katie Kazoo,
SWITCHEROO

A Collection of Katie
Books 1–4

by Nancy Krulik • illustrated by John & Wendy

Grosset & Dunlap
An Imprint of Penguin Group (USA) Inc.

GROSSET & DUNLAP
Published by the Penguin Group
Penguin Group (USA) Inc., 375 Hudson Street, New York, New York 10014, USA
Penguin Group (Canada), 90 Eglinton Avenue East, Suite 700, Toronto, Ontario
M4P 2Y3, Canada (a division of Pearson Penguin Canada Inc.)
Penguin Books Ltd., 80 Strand, London WC2R 0RL, England
Penguin Group Ireland, 25 St. Stephen's Green, Dublin 2, Ireland
(a division of Penguin Books Ltd.)
Penguin Group (Australia), 250 Camberwell Road, Camberwell,
Victoria 3124, Australia (a division of Pearson Australia Group Pty. Ltd.)
Penguin Books India Pvt. Ltd., 11 Community Centre,
Panchsheel Park, New Delhi—110 017, India
Penguin Group (NZ), 67 Apollo Drive, Rosedale, Auckland 0632,
New Zealand (a division of Pearson New Zealand Ltd.)
Penguin Books. (South Africa) (Pty.) Ltd., 24 Sturdee Avenue,
Rosebank, Johannesburg 2196, South Africa

Penguin Books Ltd., Registered Offices:
80 Strand, London WC2R 0RL, England

Text copyright © 2002, 2008 by Nancy Krulik.
Illustrations copyright © 2002, 2008 by John & Wendy. All rights reserved.
Published in 2012 by Grosset & Dunlap, a division of Penguin Young
Readers Group, 345 Hudson Street, New York, New York 10014.
GROSSET & DUNLAP is a trademark of Penguin Group (USA) Inc.
Printed in the U.S.A.

The Library of Congress has catalogued the individual books under the
following Control Numbers: 2002102949 (#1 *Anyone But Me*),
2002102953 (#2 *Out to Lunch*), 2010655078 (#3 *Oh, Baby!*),
2010655079 (#4 *Girls Don't Have Cooties*)

ISBN 978-0-448-46304-9

10 9 8 7

Katie Kazoo,
SWITCHEROO

Anyone But Me

Chapter 1

"I've got it! I've got it!"

The football soared right toward Katie Carew. She ran toward the ball, reached out her hands and . . . *oomph!* She missed it completely.

"You took your eyes off it again," Katie's best friend, Jeremy Fox, said, jogging up to her. He pushed his thin wire glasses higher up on his nose and ran his hands through his curly brown hair.

"I know," Katie replied simply. What else could she say?

"Katie, I can't believe you did that!" Kevin Camilleri shouted across the field. "You lost

1

the whole game for us."

Just then George Brennan came charging across the field. He had a big smile on his face. Katie groaned. Of course George was happy. His team had just won the game—thanks to Katie's fumble!

"Don't yell at the secret weapon," George told Kevin.

"Secret weapon? Are you kidding?" Kevin asked. "Secret weapons help *win* games, George."

"Exactly," George agreed. "Katie's the secret weapon for *our* team!"

Katie blinked her eyes tight. She didn't want George to see her cry.

"Forget about George," Jeremy whispered to Katie. "He can't help being mean. He was just born that way."

Katie tried to smile. "Could be," she said.

The truth was, Katie wasn't really sure why George was nasty to everyone in class 3A. Most new kids tried to make friends. Not

George. He tried to make enemies.

Just then, Katie's other best friend, Suzanne Lock, ran across the playground to them. "Let's go play on the monkey bars for a while," she suggested, pulling Katie and Jeremy away from George. "I'll bet I can hang upside down longer than either of you."

Katie stared at Suzanne. Her friend was wearing a skirt! "You're going to turn upside down in *that*?" Katie asked.

"Sure!" Suzanne said, yanking her skirt up to her bellybutton.

Katie's mouth flew open.

Jeremy blushed.

"It's okay, you guys," Suzanne laughed. "See, I'm wearing shorts under here. This way I can wear a skirt and still play."

Katie laughed. Leave it to Suzanne to find a way to look pretty and still hang upside down on the jungle gym.

"Okay! Last one at the monkey bars is a rotten egg," Katie called as she dashed away.

Suzanne and Jeremy took off after Katie. Katie held on to her lead, but not for long. Jeremy was the fastest runner in the class. He quickly pulled up next to Katie. Katie took a deep breath. She moved her feet faster than ever. But not fast enough. Jeremy zoomed into the lead.

Katie frowned. Well, at least she was ahead of Suzanne. Katie turned her head to see just how far behind Suzanne was and . . .

Splat!

Katie stepped right into a big, wet puddle. Gushy brown mud splashed all over her. Katie stopped running and looked down at her jeans.

"Oh, no!" she cried out. "What a mess!"

Katie wasn't kidding. She was a total mess. There were mud splatters all over her jeans. Her *favorite* jeans—the ones with the pink and blue flowers embroidered all over them.

If this were first grade, Katie could have changed into the clean clothes in her cubby. But Katie was in third grade now. Nobody in third grade kept a change of clothes at school. That was for babies. Katie was going to have to wear her mud-stained jeans for the whole rest of the day.

"Nice one, Carew," George shouted across the yard. "Check it out, everybody! There's a Mud Monster in the playground."

George stuck his arms straight out and walked around the yard pretending to be Frankenstein. The other kids laughed.

Katie wanted to cry. This was the worst recess ever. She wished Mrs. Derkman would blow her whistle and make everyone go in to class. Even doing schoolwork had to be better than this!

"George, go away or I'm gonna tell," Suzanne warned as she ran over to defend her friend.

A big smile formed on George's chubby, round face. "Yeah, like I'm real scared," he laughed while he pretended to tremble. "What's Mrs. *Jerkman* going to do? Call my mommy?"

Katie and Suzanne stared at George in

amazement. He'd just called their teacher, Mrs. Derkman, a mean name—and he hadn't even whispered it! He didn't seem scared to have the teacher phone his mom, either.

Before Katie or Suzanne could answer George, Mrs. Derkman blew her red whistle three times.

Phew! Recess was over. It was time to go back to class. Katie was very glad. She used her hands to wipe off some of the mud, and then ran to line up.

"You okay?" Jeremy whispered to Katie.

"I guess," Katie replied.

"George is a creep. You know that."

Katie nodded. But knowing that wasn't going to make George stop calling her the Mud Monster. He'd probably go at it all day, unless . . .

Katie couldn't help wishing that someone else would do something embarrassing that afternoon. Then maybe George Brennan would tease that kid instead.

Chapter 2

"This is for you," Kevin whispered to Katie. He handed her a note. It was written on light-blue paper and folded up really small. Katie knew it was from Suzanne. Her notes always looked like that.

"If you have an answer for her, send it yourself," Kevin told Katie. "I don't want to get into trouble again."

Katie understood. Kevin sat at the desk right between Suzanne and Katie. He always wound up passing notes from girl to girl. Yesterday, Mrs. Derkman had caught Kevin passing a note from Katie to Suzanne. Kevin had had to write an apology note to Mrs. Derkman.

Katie unfolded the paper. *Do you want to come over after school?* the note read.

Katie scribbled her answer on the bottom of the note. *No, thanks. I have to go home and change. Maybe tomorrow?*

Katie tossed the paper over Kevin's head. It landed right on Suzanne's desk. Katie crossed her fingers, hoping Mrs. Derkman didn't see.

Katie lucked out. Mrs. Derkman didn't notice the flying note. She was too busy writing on the board.

"Okay, take out your pencils and math notebooks. Today we're going to review subtraction with borrowing," the teacher announced.

Katie gulped. Whenever Mrs. Derkman said the word "review," it meant that she was going to ask some of the kids in the class to go to the board and solve the problems in front of everyone.

Katie slid down low in her chair, hoping

Mrs. Derkman wouldn't notice her. She didn't want to be one of the kids who were called on. It wasn't that Katie couldn't do subtraction with borrowing. It was more that she hated being in front of the whole class.

"I'll try one, Mrs. Derkman," Suzanne volunteered.

Katie sighed. Suzanne never worried about making a mistake in front of the whole class. She just liked being the center of attention. Katie wished she could be more like that.

But today, Mrs. Derkman didn't ask Suzanne to come up to the board. She picked Mandy Banks, Zoe Canter, and Jeremy instead. Mandy went first. She whizzed through her problem. No surprise there—she was like a computer when it came to math. Next it was Zoe's turn.

"All right, Zoe," Mrs. Derkman said as Zoe walked up to the board. "What will you get when you subtract 152 from 901?"

"The wrong answer!" George joked out loud.

Some kids in the class giggled. Zoe blushed.

Katie thought it was really mean of George to joke around like that. Everyone knew Zoe had a lot of trouble with math.

Mrs. Derkman looked sternly over at George, but she smiled at Zoe. "Go ahead," she said to her. "We'll do it together."

When it was his turn, Jeremy took his time solving the subtraction problem. Katie smiled. That was Jeremy: slow and steady like the tortoise in the story of *The Tortoise and the Hare.*

Sometimes Jeremy's careful slowness could get kind of annoying. But not today. *As long as Jeremy's up there, Mrs. Derkman won't call on me,* Katie thought to herself.

But eventually Jeremy did finish the problem. And he got the right answer . . . as usual.

Mrs. Derkman smiled and wrote another math problem on the board. "Let's do one more," she said.

Katie sunk even lower in her chair. Her lip was practically resting on her desk. But it was no use. Mrs. Derkman saw her anyway.

"Katie, will you solve this for us?" the teacher asked.

Katie sighed. She stood up and slowly walked toward the board.

"Here comes the Mud Monster!" Katie heard George whisper as she walked past his desk. Katie didn't want to walk past George, but she had no choice. He sat right in the front row—where Mrs. Derkman could keep an eye on him.

Katie reached the board and picked up a piece of yellow chalk. She opened her mouth to take a deep, calming breath. But instead of breathing in air, she let out a great big belch.

It was the loudest burp she'd ever heard.
A real record-breaker.

The other kids in class began to laugh.
Katie blushed beet red. "I'm sorry," she
apologized to Mrs. Derkman. Katie didn't
want her teacher to think she'd done that
on purpose.

Out of the corner of her eye, Katie could
see George holding his nose. He was pretending
to die from the smell of her breath.

"Katie's stinking up the classroom!"
George exclaimed. He laughed so hard, he
nearly fell off his chair.

Chapter 3

For the rest of that day, everywhere Katie looked, someone was laughing at her. Mostly because George kept cracking jokes.

"Hey, Mud Monster, can you burp a song for us?" he asked. "I can." George began to belch out the ABC song. By the time he got to Z, the other kids were all giggling.

"Hey, you know something?" George announced. "Burping a song kinda sounds like a kazoo. That's what your name should be, Katie. Not Katie Carew. Katie *Kazoo*!" Then he started chanting, "Katie Kazoo, Katie Kazoo," over and over again.

The other kids began to join in. "Katie

Kazoo. Katie Kazoo. Katie Kazoo. Katie Kazoo!"

Katie sank down in her chair. She tried hard not to cry.

"All right, that's enough," Mrs. Derkman scolded the class. She turned to George. "I'm sending a note home to your mother. I expect you to bring it back to me with her signature."

George shrugged as if he didn't care.

As the afternoon went on, Katie wished the other kids would stop laughing when George teased her. He really wasn't all that funny. But she did kind of understand why the kids kept laughing. If they didn't, George might make fun of them next.

Before school ended, Katie walked over toward the window, where the hamster cage was. It was her turn to feed Speedy this week.

Hamsters are so lucky, Katie thought to herself as she watched Speedy running on his wheel. *They never have bad days. Every day is just the same for them.*

Finally, the bell rang. The day was over. Katie grabbed her books and ran for the door. She had to make sure she was the first one out of the classroom.

But it didn't matter. George caught up to Katie right away. He followed her halfway home. "Katie Kazoo, I see you!" he shouted.

"Hey, Katie, wait up!"

Katie could hear Jeremy calling after her as she ran towards her house. She knew he just wanted to make her feel better. But Katie didn't stop. She didn't want to hang out with Jeremy. She just wanted to get home, go upstairs to her room, and shut the door.

Even that wasn't easy to do. When Katie got home, her mother was sitting on the front steps, waiting for her.

"Hi, Kat!" Her mother greeted her with her special nickname. "I made some yummy chocolate-chip cookies. Want some?"

"I, um, I'm not hungry right now," Katie mumbled. She raced past her and opened the screen door. "I gotta get homework done."

As Katie entered her room, she found her brown-and-white cocker spaniel, Pepper, lying on her bed. Pepper picked up his head and looked at Katie. He reached out his long, pink tongue and gave her a big kiss. Katie hugged her dog tightly.

"Thanks, Pepper," she whispered quietly into his brown floppy ear. "At least *someone* isn't making fun of me today."

Pepper looked up at her and smiled.

Jeremy was always telling Katie that dogs couldn't really smile. But Katie was sure that Pepper could. "Pepper's just a really special dog," she would tell Jeremy when he argued with her. "He's even smarter than people."

Now, as Pepper lay his head in her lap,

Katie decided that even if her cocker spaniel wasn't smarter than people, he certainly was nicer.

That night at dinner, Katie picked at her spaghetti. She rolled the long noodles around on her fork. Then she pushed the meatballs over to the side of her plate and scowled.

Three weeks ago, Katie had told her mother that she was a vegetarian. Her mother kept giving her meat anyway. Well, Katie was just not going to eat the meatballs, that's all.

"You wouldn't believe the day I had at the office," Katie's father announced as he took a bite of his meatball. "We have this new guy, and he was working on the computer when . . ."

Usually Katie hated it when her father took up the whole dinner talking about his accounting firm. But tonight she was happy to sit quietly and let him talk. It was better than having to explain why she was so miserable.

Unfortunately, her dad's story finally

came to an end. Immediately, Katie's mother changed the subject. "So, Kat, what's new with you?" she asked.

Katie shrugged. "Nothing."

"Really?" her mother asked. "Well, you sure had a lot of homework. I haven't seen you since you got home."

Katie nodded slowly. "We had a ton of social studies questions," she muttered. "Um . . . I'm not so hungry. Can I be excused?"

Katie watched as her parents gave each other their "nervous" looks. They knew something was wrong. They just weren't sure what to do about it. Finally, her mother said, "Sure, Kat. Go ahead. I'll clear the table."

Katie stood up and walked out of the room. She opened the front door, and sat on the stoop outside her house. She looked out into the darkness. Suddenly the whole rotten day flashed in front of her eyes.

She thought about missing the football and losing the game for her team.

She thought about her new jeans in the hamper, all caked with mud.

She thought about the belch she'd let out during math.

Worst of all, she thought about what George was going to do to her tomorrow.

"I wish I could be anyone but me!" she shouted out loud.

A shooting star shot across the dark night sky. But Katie was too upset to notice it.

Chapter 4

"Rise and shine, Katie! You're going to be late for school!" Katie's mother called from the kitchen.

Katie sat up slowly and rubbed the sleep from her eyes. She squinted at the Mickey Mouse clock on her wall. Mickey's hands were on the 8 and the 3. Oh no! It was already 8:15. School started at 8:45. She only had half an hour to get dressed, eat breakfast, and walk to school. This day was starting out really lousy.

Her mother had put out Katie's clothes for the day—a bright yellow satiny blouse and black jeans. The outfit was very cheerful.

But Katie wasn't feeling cheerful today. She went to her closet and pulled out a gray sweatshirt and jeans instead. That's how she felt. *Blech.* Like a gray, cloudy day.

As Katie came into the kitchen, her mother noticed her new outfit. "Not in the mood for yellow, huh kiddo?" she asked kindly.

Katie shook her head.

"Did you have an argument with Suzanne or Jeremy?" her mother guessed.

"No," Katie answered.

"So what's wrong?" her mother asked.

Katie thought about telling her mother what had happened yesterday. But she was afraid that her mom would call the school to complain about George's bullying. Imagine how mean George would be to her if *that* happened!

"Nothing's wrong," Katie lied to her mother. "I'm just tired."

Her mom didn't say anything. But Katie could tell she didn't believe her.

"You'd better eat that toast," her mom said. "It's getting late."

Katie nodded and slowly took a nibble of her bread. She slowly chewed each tiny bite until the toast practically melted in her mouth.

Katie *wanted* to be late.

If she arrived after the bell rang, the class would all be seated and doing their work by the time she got there. Mrs. Derkman would be upset that she was late. But it was worth it if she could avoid even a little bit of George's teasing. Definitely.

"You've got to get going," Katie's mother warned her. "You can eat the rest on the way."

Katie didn't say anything. She slipped on her backpack and headed for the door.

"Have a good day, kiddo," her mother called.

By the time Katie finally reached the school, everyone was inside the building. Katie stood outside by her classroom window. She watched as her classmates scrambled into their seats. Katie knew she should hurry inside. But her feet just didn't seem to want to move.

Just then, the wind began to blow. It started out as a slow and gentle breeze. But within seconds the wind was swirling round and

round like a tornado. The weird thing was that the wild wind was only blowing around Katie. The leaves on the trees weren't moving. The bushes weren't moving. Even the flag up on the flagpole wasn't moving.

What was going on? Katie was really scared. She wished she were inside. Away from this wind. She hugged herself tightly, and closed her eyes.

And then, suddenly, everything was calm again. The wind had disappeared as quickly as it had started. Katie stood perfectly still for a moment, waiting to see if it would start up again. Finally, when she was sure the storm was over, Katie slowly opened her eyes.

Everything seemed blurry. Katie blinked really hard. Nothing changed. She still couldn't see very well.

But she could smell *really* well. And her nose was twitching. Katie stood up tall and sniffed at the air. All around her were yucky smells: salami, egg salad, old sneakers. It was hard to tell where each smell was coming from. The scents were all mixing together.

Katie hadn't only become a champion smeller. She could also hear really well. *Too* well, in fact. Everyone in the classroom seemed to be shouting. All the noise was making her nervous. Katie could feel her heart beating really, really fast.

Now Katie was really scared. She wanted to

run right home. But her parents were probably at work by now. There was no one at home to take care of her. If Katie didn't show up at school, Mrs. Derkman would phone her mother for sure. Katie definitely did not want that to happen. She ran towards the classroom. She'd have to hope her sight got better.

Bam! She bashed right into a solid glass wall.

That was weird, Katie thought. *There hadn't been a glass wall there before.*

"What's going on here?" Katie cried out.

Nobody answered. All the kids in the classroom were so busy yelling, they couldn't hear Katie's cries.

"Hello!" Katie shouted. "Can anyone hear me?"

Katie began running wildly in circles. She didn't get very far before she bashed head first into another glass wall. *Ouch!* That one really hurt.

As she reached up to rub her head, Katie

noticed that her hand looked strange. This hand was small and furry. This hand had nails  that really needed to be clipped. Katie touched her face. Her cheeks felt big and round like huge empty pouches, and her face was all hairy!

Quickly, Katie looked down at her body.

"Aaah!" she cried out. "I'm naked!"

Actually, she wasn't completely naked. Her back and stomach were covered with orange-brown fur!

And that's when Katie realized what had happened. She wasn't outside anymore. She was inside—in a hamster cage. She'd become Speedy, the class hamster.

Katie tried to scream, but the only sound that came out of her mouth was a loud squeak.

Chapter 5

"Hey, look at Speedy!" Zoe Canter called out from the other side of the glass. "He's going crazy!"

Within seconds, eighteen pairs of giant eyes were peering through the glass window. They were all staring at Katie.

Katie was really confused. How could this have happened? It didn't make any sense. People didn't just turn into hamsters.

Then Katie remembered. She'd made that wish the night before. She'd said she wanted to be anyone but herself!

"Why did *this* have to be my first wish to come true?" Katie yelped. (Of course, to the kids in class 3A, her words sounded more like "Squeak, squeak squeak, squeak squeak!")

"Somebody should throw some oil on that hamster!" George exclaimed. "That'll stop his squeaking."

"Oh, George, be quiet," Suzanne told him. "Something is obviously bothering the little guy. We should try and help him."

"It figures a rat would want to help a hamster," George said. "You're both in the same family."

"Cut it out," Suzanne replied.

"Hey, Ratgirl, show us your tail," George teased.

Katie wished she could help Suzanne, but she was just a little hamster. Luckily, George had to stop when Mrs. Derkman told them all to sit back down.

"I've got to get out of this cage," Katie squeaked to herself.

The problem was that she knew there wasn't any way out. The only opening in the cage

was at the top, and that was covered by a screened lid. The lid was Mrs. Derkman's way of making sure Speedy didn't escape. Now the lid was making sure Katie didn't escape, either.

There had to be some way to get that lid off. Katie might have a hamster body now, but she still had a human brain. She was smart enough to get out of a hamster cage. She just had to come up with a plan.

Before she could think about anything, though, she had to deal with her teeth. They were feeling really long. She needed to chew on something—and fast! Quickly, Katie scampered over to a small pile of brightly colored pieces of wood.

"Ahh, that feels better." Katie sighed as she bit into a bright green chew stick. She could feel her teeth getting shorter with each nibble.

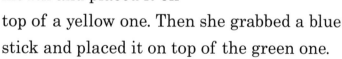

Suddenly Katie had an idea. She took the green chew stick in her mouth and placed it on top of a yellow one. Then she grabbed a blue stick and placed it on top of the green one.

If I can just build this high enough, maybe I can climb up and push the lid off, Katie thought to herself, as she took an orange chew stick and added it to the pile.

It took a while, but at last Katie built what had to be the biggest chew-stick ladder of all time. (It also was probably the *only* chew-stick ladder of all time!) If Katie could climb to the top of the pile, she might be able to reach the lid.

"Hey, look what Speedy made," she heard Manny Gonzalez whisper to Kevin.

"Cool!" Kevin agreed. "It's like a chew-stick mountain."

Katie licked her little front paws and admired her work. She took a deep breath. It was time to try out her plan. Carefully, Katie stepped onto the bottom chew stick. *So far so good,* she thought.

Once Katie was safely on the first rung of the ladder, she stood tall on her hind legs and tried to pull herself up to the next rung.

Bonk! The entire pile of chew sticks came crashing down on top of Katie's head. Luckily, the sticks were made of a soft wood. Katie wasn't hurt. And it was kind of fun eating her way out of the pile of chew sticks.

"I have to stop this!" Katie said to herself as she chewed. "I'll never get out of here if I don't stop thinking like a hamster."

The trouble was, Katie *was* a hamster. And right then she suddenly couldn't think about anything but Speedy's hamster wheel. Katie couldn't explain why she suddenly needed to run so badly. She just did. She couldn't help herself.

"Hey, this is fun," Katie squealed as her tiny paws moved faster and faster inside the wheel.

The wheel squeaked very loudly as Katie ran. The noise didn't bother Katie's sensitive hamster ears. In fact, she kind of liked it. Mrs. Derkman, on the other hand, didn't like the squeaking at all.

"Suzanne, will you please put a carrot in Speedy's cage?" Mrs. Derkman asked. "Maybe that will get him to stop running on that squeaky wheel."

"Yes, Mrs. Derkman," Suzanne said.

Katie watched as her best friend walked over, lifted the lid off the cage, and dropped in a carrot.

Katie leaped from the wheel and grabbed the treat. As she chewed the carrot, Katie looked up gratefully at Suzanne. Her friend had given Katie more than just a snack. She'd given her a great idea, too!

Chapter 6

Katie dropped the carrot and raced over to Speedy's wheel. She started running as fast as her tiny hamster feet could carry her. The wheel moved round and round. The squeaking got louder and louder.

"Excuse me, class," Mrs. Derkman said finally. "I'm going to have to take Speedy's wheel out of his cage. The noise is making it too hard to learn."

Katie heard Mrs. Derkman's footsteps come near the glass cage. Her tiny hamster heart beat quickly. This was her only chance to get free!

Mrs. Derkman took the lid from the cage.

She reached in with her hand and tried to gently ease the hamster off the wheel.

Before Mrs. Derkman could push her off, Katie leaped out and raced up her teacher's arm. Mrs. Derkman jumped back with surprise as the furry little creature scurried over her bare skin.

Katie looked from Mrs. Derkman's elbow to the floor below. It seemed very far away. But Katie knew she had no choice. She placed her little hamster paws in front of her eyes and jumped!

Thump! Katie landed hard on the cold tile floor. Her hind legs hurt a little. So did her ears. Everyone in the class seemed to be moving and shouting at once.

"Speedy's loose!" Kevin announced.

"Somebody catch him!" Zoe shouted.

"I'll get him," Jeremy volunteered. He got down on his hands and knees.

"No, I'll do it," Ricky Dobbs said. He got down on his hands and knees, too.

"I think I can get him," Mandy yelled.

Suddenly everyone seemed to be grabbing for Katie. Her little hamster body shook with fear. She was lost in a big pile of giant human hands. They were all grabbing for her. Katie couldn't let the kids catch her. They'd put her back in the cage again!

Katie ran toward the front of the room. It seemed more empty there. But as she reached Mrs. Derkman's desk, she caught a whiff of human. Whoever was standing there was covered in kid smells—spilled orange juice, crumbs, and waxy crayons.

Suddenly, the boy by the desk shrieked. "Get it away from me! Get this thing away from me!"

Katie would know that voice anywhere. It was George. She couldn't believe it! The big class bully was scared of a tiny little hamster.

Katie couldn't help herself. She ran over to George and brushed up against his leg. Then she climbed right over his shoe.

"AAAAH!" George screamed as he leaped up onto Mrs. Derkman's desk. He stood there, high off the ground, shaking. "Get it! Somebody catch that furball!" he screamed.

Katie laughed to herself. The class bully had been bullied—by a tiny little hamster. Deep down, Katie knew she'd been pretty mean. Her parents had always told her that two wrongs don't make a right, but Katie couldn't help feeling just a little bit happy at hearing George screaming in fear.

Just then, the classroom door opened.

Mr. Kane, the principal, was standing at the door. "What's going on in here?" he asked.

"Our hamster is loose," Suzanne explained quickly.

"There he goes!" Miriam added, as Katie ran right between Mr. Kane's legs and out the door.

"Hang on, Speedy!" Kevin cried out. "We'll save you!"

Chapter 7

"Not so fast, Kevin," Mr. Kane said. "I can't have a whole third-grade class running around the school."

"But we have to find Speedy," Kevin argued.

"Right now you have to go to gym class," Mrs. Derkman interrupted. "I'm sure Speedy will turn up."

"But Mrs. Derkman," Jeremy pleaded. "He could get stuck in a wall or something."

Mrs. Derkman sighed. "I'm sure he'll be fine, Jeremy. Now, class, let's line up. We're already late."

Katie raced down the hall as quickly as her little legs could take her. She was looking for someplace where she could be safe.

As she turned the corner, Katie found herself in a small empty room. What a relief! There was no one here to chase her. She stood on her hind legs and began to clean her front paws with her little pink tongue.

Just then, Katie heard footsteps coming into the room. She froze in place as someone turned on a light.

"Man, Brennan, you are such a chicken!" Katie recognized Ricky's voice. "I didn't think you would be afraid of a tiny hamster."

"I'm not," George answered him.

"So how come you were screaming like that?" Ricky continued.

"How come your face is like that?" George argued back.

It wasn't much of an answer, but it sure shut Ricky up. "I'm not afraid of anything," George continued.

Katie sniffed at the air. The room was beginning to smell like old sneakers and dirty socks.

"Do you think Coach G. will make us play kickball again?" Kevin asked. "I hate that game."

"Well, we'd better hurry up and get out there. Coach gets mad when we take too long in the locker room," Jeremy said.

Katie's eyes grew wide. Oh no! She was in the boys' locker room . . . while the boys were getting dressed for gym! This was so embarrassing!

Katie had to find a good hiding place.

Someplace where the boys couldn't see her.

Someplace where she couldn't see anything she wasn't supposed to see!

Quickly, Katie leaped into the nearest small hole. She landed in some sort of strange, soft cave. She crept inside as far as she could go. Then she sat very, very still.

The inside of the cave was moist and

stinky. It smelled like sweaty feet. But at least it was dark and quiet. No one would find her here.

Suddenly, Katie felt someone lift her hiding place right off the floor. Katie peeked out and looked up. A giant, stinky gym sock was coming right at her!

Yikes!

Katie's safe cave was actually someone's sneaker. And whoever the sneaker belonged to was about to crush her with his big, smelly foot!

Katie had to escape from her sneaker cave. She ran toward the opening, and leaped out onto the floor.

"AAAAHHHH!" George screamed as he dropped his sneaker. "There's a mouse in my shoe!" He leaped up on a bench. "Get it out of here!"

"That's no mouse," Ricky yelled. "That's Speedy!"

"We've got to get him," Manny Gonzalez shouted.

But Katie wasn't about to be caught in the boys' locker room. She ran for the door.

The boys' screams were way in the distance by the time Katie felt safe enough to stop running. She hid behind a trash can and stood very, very still. She was trying to hear if anyone was coming after her. Luckily, the hallway was silent.

Suddenly a wind began to blow. Katie lifted her little hamster nose and tried to sniff at the breeze. She didn't smell anything unusual— just the ammonia that the janitor, Mr. Peterson, used to clean the floor. She couldn't smell any flowers, trees, or even car fumes coming from outside the school. In fact, there didn't seem to be a window open anywhere.

Still, the wind was definitely blowing. Katie could feel it whipping through her thick, orange fur. It swirled all around her like a tornado . . . exactly as it had just before Katie had turned into a hamster!

Oh no! Katie thought. *What's happening to me now?*

Chapter 8

Finally, the magical wind stopped blowing. But Katie was afraid to open her eyes. She'd already been turned into a hamster. What if this time she were something even worse— like an ant or something?

Slowly, Katie cracked open one eye. She raised her hands to her face. No fur. Good. And she had fingers—five of them on each hand. She looked at her nails. They were filed short. A few of them still showed a few chips of leftover glow-in-the-dark glitter nail polish. These were definitely her hands.

Was it possible? Had she turned back into herself?

Quickly, Katie ran into the girls' room and looked in the mirror. An eight-year-old girl with red hair, green eyes, and a line of freckles across her nose looked back at her. It was true! Katie was back!

Out of the corner of her eye, Katie saw a small orange ball of fluff rush past her into

one of the bathroom stalls. Speedy! The real
Speedy was really on the loose. Quickly she
ran into the stall. She found Speedy hiding
behind the toilet. He seemed frightened and
confused.

Katie scooped the hamster up and held
him in her hands. "It's okay, little guy," she
told him quietly. "Everything's back to
normal now."

As Katie walked back to the gym, the voices
of her friends became
louder. They were all
complaining because
Coach G. and Mrs.
Derkman wouldn't
let them chase after
Speedy. Katie grinned
as she opened the
gym door. She
would be a hero
for bringing the
hamster back.

"Were you guys looking for this?" she asked as she walked in the door.

"Katie, where'd you find him?" Suzanne shouted from the other side of the room.

"Oh, we just sort of ran into each other in the girls' room," Katie replied.

"Boy, it was a good thing you were late today," Kevin told her. "Otherwise Speedy might have been gone forever."

"It's never a good thing to be late for school, Kevin," Mrs. Derkman reminded him. "But I am glad you found the hamster, Katie. Now, please put take him back to the classroom and put him in his cage. And make sure the lid is on tightly."

Katie did as she was told. She pet Speedy gently as she placed him down on his cage floor. Then she handed him a treat bar.

"You deserve this," she whispered quietly. "We worked really hard this morning."

Speedy slept for the rest of the morning. Katie spent the time trying to keep her mind on her lessons. But it was hard for her to think about anything other than her adventure. After all, how often does an eight-year-old girl turn into a hamster?

Katie wished she could tell Jeremy and Suzanne all about what had happened to her. But she knew they would never believe her. She wouldn't believe it either if it hadn't happened to her.

This was one secret Katie would have to keep to herself.

"Boy, did you pick the wrong morning to be late," Jeremy told Katie as they walked out onto the playground after lunch. "It was so weird. Speedy was out of his mind. I'd never seen him like that!"

"I'd never seen George like that either," Suzanne giggled. "I can't believe you missed it, Katie. He was terrified of a little hamster. What a wimp!"

"I can't believe we were ever scared of

George," Miriam agreed.

"I was never afraid of him," Kevin argued.

Jeremy rolled his eyes. "So how come you walk three blocks out of your way to get to school—just so you don't have to pass his house on the way?"

Kevin blushed.

The kids looked over at George. He was sitting on a bench all by himself. He didn't look mean anymore. He just looked lonely.

"Hey, George!" Manny Gonzalez called out. "Why did the hamster cross the road?"

George didn't answer. He obviously didn't want to talk about hamsters.

"Because it was the chicken's day off!" Manny finished off his own joke. Then he waited for George to say something mean to him.

But George didn't say anything. He just scowled and turned away. For the first time, the other kids were doing the teasing. George didn't like that at all.

"Well, I guess we don't have to be afraid of George anymore," Jeremy said to the others.

Suzanne nodded. "We have Speedy to thank for that."

Katie smiled to herself. She knew that class 3A actually had her to thank for stopping George's bullying. She was a real hero.

Chapter 9

Katie was in a great mood when she got home that afternoon. Pepper met her at the steps. Katie bent down and gave her cocker spaniel a huge hug.

Pepper licked her on the nose.

"Well, I'm glad to see you're happy again," Katie's mother said as she came out of the house with two glasses of pink lemonade. "You just weren't yourself this morning."

Katie laughed. Her mother didn't know the half of it.

"So, did anything exciting happen at school today?" her mother asked.

Katie almost choked on her lemonade. It

was only the most exciting—and scary—day of her whole life! But Katie couldn't tell her mother that. Instead she said, "Our hamster got loose, and I caught him!"

"Good for you!" her mother said. Then she shuddered. "I can't imagine having a hamster running loose around a classroom. I don't really like little rodents like that."

"Oh, you'd like Speedy, Mom. I know you would." Katie finished off her drink.

"So, what do you want to do this afternoon?" Katie's mom asked as she sipped slowly at her drink. "You want to come inside and have some cookies before you start your homework?"

Katie shook her head. "We don't have a whole lot of homework today. Just a current events worksheet. So can Pepper and I go for a walk?"

"I don't see why not," her mother said. "You can do the worksheet after dinner. I'll put the newspaper up in your room."

Katie handed her mom the empty glass and jumped up.

"Come on, Pepper!" she called out. "Let's walk!"

Katie never thought she'd be so happy just to walk around on two legs. But it felt great to stand straight and tall. She loved being able to run wherever she wanted, not just on some silly, squeaky wheel. Katie did a big cartwheel, right in the middle of the sidewalk.

Unfortunately, Katie was not very good at cartwheels. Instead of landing on her feet, she landed— *splat*—right on her rear end.

As Katie stood up, she noticed a boy about her age sitting alone on his front porch. He was wearing dark sunglasses and a baseball hat. At first she didn't recognize him. Then the boy called out, "You okay?"

It was George Brennan. A nervous feeling came over Katie. Was George going to make fun of her for falling down?

"I said, are you okay?"

Katie stood up and brushed off her jeans. "Yeah, I'm fine. Thanks." She looked at George. He seemed more embarrassed than she was. He seemed kind of sad, too.

For the first time, Katie felt a little sorry for George. At least when George had made fun of her for falling in the mud, she'd had friends to cheer her up. George had no one.

"Is this your house?" she asked him nervously.

"No, I just like to sit on other people's porches," George snapped back, making a nasty joke. "Of course it's my house."

Katie turned and began to walk away. If George was going to be mean, she wasn't going to talk to him.

"Hey, is that your dog?" George called after her.

Katie stopped walking. She turned around and smiled. "No, I just like hanging out with other people's dogs," she joked back. "Of course he's my dog."

George smiled—a little bit. "Good one," he admitted.

Katie smiled back. "His name's Pepper. You want to pet him? Or are you afraid of dogs, too?"

George blushed. "Never mind."

Katie felt bad. She hadn't been teasing. She really didn't know if George had a problem with all animals, or just hamsters.

"No, I mean it," she assured him. "If you were afraid of dogs, it wouldn't be such a bad thing. A lot of people are afraid dogs will bite or something. But Pepper wouldn't do that."

"I'm not afraid of dogs," George told her. "I'm not even afraid of hamsters. This morning I was just sort of goofing on all the kids who were afraid of Speedy. You weren't there. You should have seen them all crying and screaming and stuff."

Katie knew that was a lie. None of the other kids were afraid of Speedy. They were all trying to catch the hamster. The only kid crying and jumping on chairs was George.

But Katie didn't tell George that. He'd only wonder how she knew what was going on in the classroom, since the whole class thought she was late for school today. Besides, George must have felt really embarrassed about being afraid of hamsters. Why else would he lie about it?

"Oh, I guess everyone else got it wrong," Katie told him, trying to be nice.

"I guess," George mumbled.

"So, you want to pet my dog then?" Katie asked.

"Okay," George said quietly.

Katie walked Pepper up toward George's house. George reached his hand out slowly. It was obvious that he was nervous around dogs, too, but he wasn't going to admit it to Katie. Pepper sat on his hind legs and lifted his head. When George gave Pepper a little pat, the dog licked George's hand. George wrinkled up his nose. He wasn't used to dog kisses.

"He's a pretty cool dog," George admitted.

"Thanks," Katie replied, sitting down next to George. "You know, it's okay to be afraid of something."

George frowned. "Oh yeah, right. So what are you afraid of?"

"I *was* afraid of you—at least until today," Katie admitted.

George smiled. He seemed almost proud of the fact that Katie had been scared of him.

"So you're not afraid of me anymore, huh?" he asked her finally.

Katie shook her head. "Nope."

"I guess none of the kids are scared of me after today," George moaned.

"Why would you want us to be scared of you?" Katie asked.

George shrugged. "Just because."

"I don't know why you have to make mean jokes all the time," Katie said.

"I make jokes so that people will laugh," George told her. "I'd rather have people laugh

at my jokes than laugh at me."

"Why do you think people will laugh at you?" Katie asked him.

George looked at her and rolled his eyes. "Are you kidding? I'm the new kid. Everyone makes fun of the new kid. They laugh at the way the new kid talks, and the clothes the new kid wears. This is the third school I've been to since kindergarten. My dad has had to switch jobs three times. But you know what? After today, I wish my family could move again."

"Don't say that!" Katie exclaimed. "Don't make wishes you don't really mean. You never know when they'll come true."

"But I'm miserable here," George said. "All the kids hate me. And now they won't even laugh at my jokes."

Katie thought about that for a minute. Then she had an idea. "Don't you know any jokes that aren't mean?" Katie asked George. "You can still make kids laugh without making them feel bad."

"I don't know," George answered. "I've never thought about jokes that weren't mean."

"I have a bunch of joke books at my house. Do you want to come over and look at some of them? You can try the jokes out on the kids at school tomorrow."

George didn't say anything at first. Then he looked sort of embarrassed. "I'm sorry I kept calling you Katie Kazoo," he said finally.

Katie grinned. "It's okay. I kind of like it, actually."

"You do?" George asked.

Katie nodded. "It's a pretty cool nickname. It's the kind of name Suzanne would give herself—if she could."

George looked at Katie. "How come you're being nice to me?" he demanded.

Katie shrugged. "I guess because you're being nice to me," she said simply.

Chapter 10

The next morning Katie was up and dressed before her parents awoke. She wanted to be sure to get to school before George did. Katie had a feeling that the other kids were going to make fun of George for being afraid of Speedy. If they did, he might be mean right back to them. Then he would never make friends at school.

Katie really wanted to help George. They had spent a lot of time laughing at joke books together yesterday afternoon. George was really an okay kid. Katie hoped the other kids could see that side of him.

Besides, Katie figured that if George made

friends with the kids at school, he wouldn't want to make fun of them. School would be a lot more fun if everybody wasn't always afraid that George would say something mean to them. So, by helping George, Katie was helping all the other kids, too.

If her plan worked, Katie would be a hero two days in a row!

Katie got to the schoolyard ten minutes early. She sat down on a bench and waited for her friends—and George—to arrive.

"You're here early," Suzanne said a few minutes later, plopping down onto the bench beside Katie.

The key chains on Suzanne's backpack jingled and jangled as the pack hit the ground. Suzanne had a stretchy-alien key chain, a Slinky dog key chain, a key chain that looked like a Barbie doll, and key chains from Vermont, Texas, and California. She even had a key chain with a mirror on it.

Katie only had two key chains on her back-pack. One was a photo frame with a picture of Pepper in it. The other one was a little rubber monkey that bounced up and down when you shook it.

"Are you trying to make up for being late yesterday?" Suzanne asked.

Katie shook her head. "I'm just waiting."

"For what?"

Katie shrugged. "Oh, nothing."

By now Jeremy and Kevin were there, too. Miriam's mother pulled up in her car. Miriam and Mandy leaped out of the backseat. Manny rode up on his bicycle. He locked the ten-speeder to the bike rack and walked over toward the other kids.

Katie looked around. Most of the kids in her class were there. Now she just had to wait for George.

Katie glanced at her watch. School was starting in five minutes. What if George was afraid to show up? The other kids would be sure he was absent because of Speedy. They'd never let him live that down.

Finally, she saw George walking up the hill toward the schoolyard. He was walking very slowly, but he was definitely coming.

"How come you're so late, George?" Katie asked as George joined the group.

"My clock was slow," George replied. "You'd be slow too, if you'd been running all night."

Katie and George looked at each other nervously.

And then the worst thing happened. Nobody laughed. NOBODY. The kids just stood there staring at George.

George blushed red. He looked angrily at Katie.

Katie gulped. This was not good.

Quickly, Katie tried to get George to tell another joke. A funnier one this time.

"Don't you wish this was the last day of school, George?" she asked him.

The kids all stared at Katie. Why was she being so nice to George Brennan?

"You know, Katie, there is one school you have to drop out of before you can graduate," George began.

"What school is that?" Katie asked.

"Parachute school," George told her.

Again, nobody laughed. Now Katie was getting really worried.

And then, out of nowhere, Jeremy started

laughing—really hard. He was totally cracking up. The other kids looked at him in amazement.

Jeremy stared back at them. "What?" he asked. "It was funny."

"Thanks," George said. He sounded a little happier now.

"Tell another one," Katie urged.

"Okay," George agreed. "What's the most important subject a witch learns in school?"

"What?" Katie asked.

"Spelling!" George answered.

Jeremy started laughing again. So did Suzanne. Suddenly all the kids were giggling at George's joke.

"That was a good one," Kevin said. "Got any more jokes?"

George's face broke into a smile. A real, happy smile, not the mean smile he usually had on his face. "Sure, I've got a million of 'em." He looked around at the other kids. "Why didn't the skeleton do well in school?"

"Why?" Suzanne asked.

"Because his heart wasn't in it!" George said.

Everyone started laughing all over again.

"Wait, wait! Here's another one!" George announced. "What's the hardest part about taking a test?"

"What?" asked Mandy.

"The answers!" George told her.

George was on a roll. He couldn't stop telling jokes. That was a good thing, since the kids didn't want him to stop. "What table doesn't have any legs?" he asked Jeremy.

Jeremy thought for a minute, but he couldn't guess. "I don't know," he said finally.

"A multiplication table!" George shouted out.

Once again the kids all started giggling.

Just then, Mrs. Derkman blew her whistle. "Line up, class 3A!" she called out. The kids ran to line up. Katie found herself standing right in front of George. Just one day ago, that would have been an awful place to stand.

But now, Katie didn't mind standing near George at all.

"Hey, Katie Kazoo, what do you have for lunch?" George whispered into Katie's ear.

"I'm going to buy something from the cafeteria," she whispered back. "My mom gave me lunch money today."

"I have peanut butter and Marshmallow Fluff," George said. "My mom hardly ever gives me lunch money."

"You're lucky," Katie said. "The food in the cafeteria stinks. I'd much rather have peanut butter and Marshmallow Fluff."

"We could sit together in the cafeteria and share," George suggested. "I'll give you half of my sandwich if you'll give me half of your dessert."

Katie grinned. "It's a deal!"

As class 3A walked toward the school building, Katie felt a cool breeze blow through her hair. She got a scared feeling in the pit of her stomach. Was this the same wind that had turned her into a hamster yesterday? What was going to happen to her now?

Then Katie noticed that everyone else's hair was blowing around too. This wasn't some sort of magic wind. It was just a normal, everyday breeze—the kind that cools you down without turning you into someone else.

Still, Katie had a feeling she hadn't seen the last of the magic wind. It was bound to start blowing again sometime. So the only question was . . . who was she going to turn into next?

Fun Facts About Hamsters!

If you're like Katie and
have a hamster in your
classroom, here are some
fun facts about your furry
friend.

Did you know that:

Hamsters need glasses? Hamsters are very
near-sighted. Depending on the breed, they
can usually see only a few inches or a few feet
in front of themselves.

Hamster teeth never stop growing? They
just keep getting longer and longer—unless
you give your hamster something to gnaw on,
like a wooden chew stick. When hamsters
chew, they keep their teeth short and healthy.

Hamsters need lots of exercise? In the wild,
hamsters may travel several miles a night in
search of food. Hamsters that are kept as pets
need the same amount of exercise, which is

why they run on their wheels.

Hamsters squeak to get your attention?
Hamsters usually make squeaking noises
when they want more food or attention.

Hamsters sometimes eat their poop? As
gross as it may sound, hamsters sometimes do
just that. Their digestive systems are different
than ours. Some hamster poop contains cer-
tain nutrients that the hamster needs.

Hamsters don't need shampoo? All hamsters know how to clean themselves. They
don't need fancy sponges and shampoo to do
it either. Hamsters groom themselves by licking
their coat at the back and the front. They also
lick their paws and then rub their paws over
their face and behind their ears. They do that
because they can't actually lick their faces.

Some hamsters take baths in dry sand?
Hamsters love rolling around in sand. The
sand takes some of the grease off of their
skin. That makes them feel more comfortable.
If you have a hamster, you might want to put

a dish of sand in the cage for the hamster to
roll around in.

Katie Kazoo, SWITCHEROO

Out to Lunch

Chapter 1

"How many tomatoes are you going to eat?" Katie Carew asked her friend Kevin Camilleri as she plopped down into the seat across from him in the school cafeteria. Kevin had opened his lunch box. Inside were all sorts of tomatoes—tiny grape tomatoes; small, round cherry tomatoes; oval-shaped plum tomatoes; and a big plastic bag filled with sliced tomatoes. And for dessert, he had a bag of tomato-flavored chips.

Kevin picked up one of the oval-shaped tomatoes and bit into it like an apple. "I could probably eat about a million of these. I love tomatoes!"

All the kids at the table laughed. They knew that Kevin had been a tomato freak since kindergarten. Back then they had even nicknamed him Tomato Man.

"You've never met a tomato you didn't like, right, Kevin?" Katie teased.

"That's not true," Kevin said. "I'd never eat a tomato from the school salad bar."

The kids at the table agreed. The vegetables at the salad bar were pretty gross.

"Hey, how do you stop a rotten tomato from smelling?" George Brennan asked, dropping his tray down next to Katie. George loved jokes and riddles. He told them all the time.

"How?" Kevin asked him.

"Hold its nose!" George answered. He began laughing hysterically. He turned to Katie. "Good one, huh, Katie Kazoo?"

Katie giggled. She loved George's jokes. She didn't even mind when he called her Katie Kazoo. She thought the nickname sounded sort of cool! She'd even tried signing

Katie Kazoo on her schoolwork—until her teacher, Mrs. Derkman, made her write her real name on her papers.

"Whoops," Katie knocked her spoon off the table when she laughed. "Hold my place George," she told him. "I'll be right back."

Katie got up from the table and walked over to the lunch counter. "May I have a spoon?" she asked the lunch lady.

"Didn't you get one already?" the lunch lady answered in a very grouchy voice.

"I dropped it," Katie explained.

"Tough toenails," the lunch lady told her. "One spoon per customer."

"But how am I going to eat my pudding?"

The lunch lady rolled her eyes. "Use your hands. Or better yet, don't eat it at all. I wouldn't."

The lunch lady hadn't been very nice. But she was probably right. The pudding looked disgusting, and it smelled worse. Katie *was* better off not eating it.

Katie went back to the lunch table. She sat down and looked at her apple. If she ate around the rotten spot, it might be okay.

"Got room over here for me?" Suzanne Lock asked.

Katie scooted over to make room for her best friend. Suzanne put down her cafeteria tray and sat beside Katie.

"I thought you were sitting at the other

table with Jeremy," Katie said. She looked over at the long table in the corner, where Jeremy Fox sat with two boys from the other third grade class. Katie had known Jeremy and Suzanne practically since they were babies. Jeremy and Suzanne were pals, but they didn't think of each other as best friends. Katie considered both of them her best friends, though.

"Jeremy's looking at some dumb baseball book," Suzanne explained. "It's soooo boring!" She placed her spoon into her bowl of

alphabet soup and fished around. A moment later, she lifted the spoon and smiled.

"Look! I spelled rat!"

Katie looked onto Suzanne's spoon. Sure enough, the letters R, A, and T were sitting in a sea of light orange water.

Katie giggled.

Suzanne put the spoon in her mouth and

made a funny face. "Even a rat wouldn't eat this stuff," she said. "It's terrible—just water with food coloring! It has no flavor at all."

Katie nodded. "I know what you mean. The food in this cafeteria is awful, and almost everything is made with some sort of meat. All I ever get to eat for lunch is a stale bagel and Jell-O."

"Oh, come on, Katie. Sometimes they serve gloppy, overcooked macaroni and cheese and old carrot sticks," Suzanne teased. "You can eat that."

"Yuck!" Katie exclaimed.

"That's what you get for being a vegetarian." Kevin told Katie.

"Did you hear the one about the guy with carrot sticks stuck in his ears?" George interrupted.

Katie shook her head. "No."

"That's okay," George shrugged. "He didn't hear it either!"

As George laughed at his own joke,

Suzanne frowned. "That one was really bad, George," she said. She turned back to Katie. "The fried chicken nuggets aren't too bad, and they serve those a lot. I don't know why you won't even eat a piece of chicken once in a while."

"I told you, I won't eat anything that had a face," Katie explained.

"But chickens have *ugly* faces," Kevin pointed out.

"I won't eat any animals," Katie insisted. "Of course, that doesn't leave me with many choices in the cafeteria."

"Why don't you ask your mom to pack your lunches?" Miriam Chan suggested as she took a bite of a turkey sandwich her mother had packed.

"She doesn't have time," Katie explained. "On the days she opens the store, she leaves for work at the same time I leave for school. Our house is crazy in the mornings." Katie's mom worked part time at The Book Nook, a small bookstore in the Cherrydale Mall.

"Well, I'm glad my mom packs my lunch," Kevin said. "That way, I don't ever have to face the *Lunch Lady*!" He made a scary face.

"You know what happened to me today?" Suzanne said. "I asked the lunch lady if I could have a banana that wasn't totally brown and mushy. You know what she told me? She said, 'If you want fresh fruit, get it from home. Brown mushy bananas are what's on the cafeteria menu today.' "

"She's such a grump!" Kevin said.

"You'd be grumpy too if you had to dish out smelly, disgusting food all day," Katie told him.

"That's true," Suzanne agreed.

"Speaking of disgusting, look at George!" Zoe Canter exclaimed. "I think I'm gonna throw up!"

Katie looked over at George's tray. It was totally gross. George had mixed his mashed potatoes and vegetable soup together. Then he'd poured his chocolate milk into the mix. Now he was busy stirring in some orange Jell-O.

"Hey, Katie Kazoo, do you dare me to eat this?" he asked her.

Katie made a face. "Yuck!" she exclaimed.

Suzanne stood and picked up her tray. "Come on, Katie," she said. "Let's get out of here before George really does eat that mess."

As Katie and Suzanne headed toward the playground for recess, Suzanne looked back at George and sighed. "Boys can be so dumb," she remarked.

Katie shrugged. Some boys could be pretty

dumb. But other boys were really cool. Like Jeremy. Katie was about to say that, but she stopped herself. Suzanne got mad whenever Katie talked about Jeremy. Suzanne didn't like to think that Katie had two best friends.

"Come on, hurry up!" Suzanne urged Katie. "Let's see if we can get to the hopscotch game before the fourth-graders do!"

Katie followed her friend out the door.

Katie tossed her stone toward the hopscotch board. It landed in the middle of the three. Quickly Katie began jumping up and down the board. As she bent down to pick up her stone on the way back, she heard Jeremy's voice over her head.

"You guys want to throw the ball around a little bit?" he asked.

Katie hopped off the board and smiled at Jeremy. "Maybe later," she said. "We're kind of in the middle of a game."

Suzanne gave a deep sigh. "He can see

that, Katie." She turned to Jeremy. "Can't you?"

Jeremy nodded. "I just thought maybe you two would want to play catch, that's all. You said you wanted to work on your aim," he reminded Katie.

"I do," Katie said kindly. "How about after we finish with hopscotch?"

Jeremy shrugged and pushed his glasses further up on his nose. "Sure. See ya later."

As Jeremy walked off, Katie looked at Suzanne. "You sounded kind of angry. Are you mad at Jeremy or something?" she asked.

Suzanne shook her head. "No. I just thought it was really rude of him to try to break up our game."

Katie nodded. "I guess we could have asked him if he wanted to play with us instead."

"He wouldn't have wanted to play hop-scotch," Suzanne told Katie. "None of the boys play hopscotch anymore."

Katie shrugged. Suzanne was probably

right. But they could have asked Jeremy to play anyway, just to be nice.

Just then Mandy Banks came strolling over. Miriam and Zoe were right behind her. They were each carrying flat, smooth stones—perfect for hopscotch.

"Can we play with you?" Mandy asked.

Suzanne smiled brightly. "Sure. You're right after Katie, Mandy. Then Zoe, then Miriam. This game is for third-grade girls only . . . right Katie?"

Katie didn't answer. She didn't like it when games were just for girls or just for boys. She was much happier when everybody got to play. Katie tucked her red hair behind her ears. Then she reached out and tossed her stone toward the square with the four in it. The small rock soared right over the box, and landed on the eight instead.

"Your turn, Mandy," Suzanne called out cheerfully.

Chapter 2

Classroom 3A was a wild place after lunch.

"Look out, incoming plane," George shouted as he threw a paper airplane toward Kevin.

Kevin laughed. "Back at ya!" He tossed the plane back to George.

Suzanne ducked as the paper plane shot over her head. "Hey! Watch it!" she shouted at Kevin.

"That's enough now," Mrs. Derkman told the class. "Recess is over. Please take out your writer's notebooks. We're going to work on our biographies."

Katie smiled. She loved writing biographies. Right now she was working on one about her dog, Pepper. Katie had taken care of him since he was a puppy. Pepper was like a brother to her—even better because Pepper didn't argue or ask to share her toys.

Squeak. Squeak. Squeak. Katie looked over toward the class hamster's cage. Boy, did Speedy's wheel need oiling.

Mrs. Derkman must have heard the squeaking, too, because she said, "Oh, class, before I forget—the classroom floors are being cleaned this weekend. I will need someone to take Speedy home. If you're interested, bring me a note from your parents saying it's okay."

Katie knew she couldn't even think about bringing Speedy home for the weekend—not with Pepper living there. Dogs and hamsters didn't always get along so well.

Still, Katie really wished she could take Speedy home. She cared about him more than anyone else in the whole class. Maybe that was because Katie was the only one in the class who had actually been Speedy.

It was true! Katie had actually turned into the class hamster for a whole morning!

It happened a few weeks ago. After a really, really bad day, Katie had made the mistake of wishing she could be anyone but herself.

There must have been some sort of shooting star flying through the sky at the very moment Katie had made the wish, because it had come true. (And everyone knows when you make a wish on a shooting star, it comes true!) The only thing was, 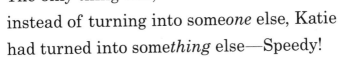 instead of turning into someone else, Katie had turned into something else—Speedy!

Katie shivered a little as she remembered being a hamster. It was really scary. She thought she'd be stuck in that tiny, smelly glass cage forever. But eventually she'd gotten loose. And luckily, once she was free, Katie had somehow turned back into herself.

Katie didn't understand how any of it had happened. All she knew was that she was really glad to be an eight-year-old girl again.

Ever since she'd spent time in Speedy's body, Katie had taken great care of the little hamster. She always made sure his water bowl was full, gave him plenty of chew sticks, and brought him fresh carrots from home.

Of course, Katie had never told anyone about turning into Speedy. She didn't think they would believe her. She wouldn't have believed it if it hadn't happened to her.

"Hey, Katie Kazoo, if I took Speedy home, you know what I would do with him?" George whispered from the desk next to Katie's.

"What?" Katie whispered back.

"Keep him in the refrigerator," George answered.

Katie looked at George with surprise. "Why would you do that?"

"To keep him from getting spoiled," George told her. "Nobody likes a spoiled hamster!"

Katie smiled and sighed. She knew George was only joking. George would never take Speedy home. He was afraid of hamsters!

As soon as the school bell rang, Katie packed up her backpack and hurried toward the door. She couldn't wait to get out of the school. It had been a very long afternoon.

Jeremy and Katie met up on the school's front steps. "I'm definitely asking my mother if I can take Speedy home," he announced.

Katie smiled. She knew how badly Jeremy wanted a pet. His mother kept saying she was waiting to see if he was responsible enough to care for one. "Great!" Katie exclaimed. "Once your mom sees how you feed Speedy, give him water, and change the dirty litter in his cage, she'll get you your own pet for sure."

"I have to change the litter?" Jeremy asked, scrunching up his nose.

"Of course," Katie told him. "Otherwise, it starts to stink!"

Before Jeremy could answer, Suzanne

came bounding down the steps toward them. "I'm so excited!" she announced.

"How come?" Katie asked her.

" 'Cause I'm going to ask my mom to let me bring Speedy home this weekend. It'll be so much fun to have him there. I'm going to build him a whole hamster playground. I can use toilet paper tubes, egg cartons, and . . . "

"Wait a minute," Jeremy interrupted her. "*You're* not bringing Speedy home."

"Why not?" Suzanne asked.

"Because *I'm* bringing him home," he told her.

"Are not!" Suzanne exclaimed.

"Am, too!" Jeremy shouted back.

"Yeah, who says?" Suzanne demanded.

"I do!" Jeremy yelled.

Suzanne looked straight at Katie. "Which one of us do *you* think Speedy should go home with?" she asked.

Katie wasn't sure what to say. As she looked from Jeremy to Suzanne, she wasn't

sure who Speedy would be happier with.
Jeremy promised he would take good care of
Speedy, but Katie knew Jeremy had a Little
League game on Saturday. What if he was so
busy thinking about baseball that he forgot to
feed Speedy?

On the other hand, Suzanne might not be

able to take care of Speedy very well, either. Suzanne's mom had just had a new baby. Now that little Heather had arrived, things were really crazy at Suzanne's house. People were always stopping by to see the new baby, and everyone was busy running around, changing diapers and heating up bottles. What if someone knocked the lid off of Speedy's cage by accident? The hamster would be long gone before anyone in her house even realized he'd escaped.

"Come on, Katie, who do you think should get to take Speedy home?" Suzanne asked Katie again.

Katie had a sick feeling in her stomach. No matter what she said, somebody would be mad at her. So, instead of making a decision, Katie walked away. "I have to get home and feed Pepper," she told her friends quickly. "Talk to you later."

Chapter 3

The next day there was trouble in room 3A. Jeremy and Suzanne both came to school with notes from their parents saying they could bring Speedy home for the weekend. Katie hoped that Mrs. Derkman would just pick one kid or the other to take the hamster. But that's not what the teacher decided to do.

"You two will have to work this out between you," Mrs. Derkman told Jeremy and Suzanne. "You have until the end of the week to tell me what you decide."

Katie thought that was just about the most terrible thing her teacher could have done. Neither Jeremy nor Suzanne was going to give in. It didn't seem like her friends even cared about taking care of Speedy anymore. All they cared about was winning.

The whole class was caught up in the war between Suzanne and Jeremy. All the boys were siding with Jeremy. The girls were all on Suzanne's side—except Katie. She didn't know whose side to be on. Jeremy and Suzanne were both her best friends.

Unfortunately, Jeremy and Suzanne weren't friends with each other anymore.

"You're going to sit with me, aren't you, Katie?" Suzanne asked as class 3A walked into the cafeteria.

"Who says she's gonna sit with you?" Jeremy interrupted. "She was my friend before she ever met you."

Suzanne rolled her eyes. "That's just because your moms knew each other when they were kids," she explained. "You guys probably wouldn't have become friends if it weren't for that."

George pulled a bag of potato chips from his lunch bag. "Do you know why best friends are like potatoes?" he asked jokingly.

"No, why?" Katie said.

"Because they're always there when the *chips* are down!" George started to laugh. "Get it?"

Katie smiled. She was glad George was trying to make everyone laugh. "That was funny," she told him.

Suzanne put her arm around Katie. "Katie's like that," she told the others. "She's always on *my* side."

Jeremy moved closer toward Katie. "No, she's always on my side," he argued.

Katie could feel the tears starting to build

up in her eyes. This just wasn't fair. "Look, you guys, I like both of you. I don't want to have to choose. I wish I could just cut myself in half," she said.

George started to laugh.

"What's so funny about that?" Katie demanded.

"Nothing." George shrugged. "It's just that I was thinking, if you cut your left side off, you'd be *all right*." He laughed again.

But for once Katie didn't laugh with him. She felt like nothing was going to be alright ever again. Quickly she turned and ran back into the hall. "I have to go to the bathroom," she mumbled as she darted away.

Katie walked into the girls' room and looked around. There was no one else there. It was nice to be alone. Maybe she could just stay in the bathroom until lunch was over. That way she could keep away from Suzanne, Jeremy, and everyone else in her class.

Katie looked at her watch. It was 12:05. Lunch was over at 1:00. That meant she would have to stay in the girls' room for fifty-five minutes. That was a very long time. What could she do in the bathroom for fifty-five minutes? Katie looked at her watch again. Make that fifty-four minutes. The hands on her watch had just moved to 12:06.

Well, for starters, she could wash her face and hands. Katie turned on the water and held her hands under the faucet.

Suddenly Katie felt a light wind blowing on her back. She looked up toward the bathroom window. It was closed. So was the door. The wind wasn't coming from outside. It was only blowing in the girls room. Katie gulped as she looked around her. The wind didn't even seem to be blowing anywhere else in the room—just around Katie.

The wind grew stronger and stronger, swirling around her like a tornado. For a minute Katie was sure it was going to lift her right off the ground—like Dorothy in *The Wizard of Oz*. She closed her eyes and grabbed on to the sink, trying to keep herself from flying away.

Katie was really scared. She knew what

trouble this kind of wind could cause. This
wasn't the first time Katie had been trapped
in a strange, magical windstorm. It had happened to her twice before, once when she'd
turned into Speedy, and once when she'd

turned back into herself. This wind could only mean one thing.

Katie Carew was becoming somebody else!

But who?

Or *what*?

After a few seconds, the wind stopped. Everything was quiet—and different. There was a really bad stink in the air. Not a bathroom stink, though. It smelled more like spoiled milk.

"Ow!" Katie yanked her hand from the sink. The cool plaster had suddenly turned really hot.

Where was she?

She slowly opened her eyes and looked nervously toward the mirror. It was time to find out just who she'd changed into.

But as Katie's eyelids fluttered open, she discovered there was no mirror in front of her. There was no sink, either. Katie wasn't even in the bathroom. She was in the cafeteria! She'd just burned her hand on the hot lunch counter.

A really bad smell began to waft up from the table.

"Yuck! What stinks?" Katie said aloud.

She looked down at a stack of disgusting gray hamburgers. Beside the burgers was a pile of old slices of American cheese. One of the slices was covered in green mold. Spoiled cheese and bad hamburgers—Katie felt sick.

Beads of sweat began to form on her forehead. Katie raised her hand to wipe them away. That's when she saw that her hands were much larger than usual—the size of adult hands. She was also wearing clear plastic gloves that made her big hands feel hot and sweaty.

Katie ran her gloved hands over her dress. The dress was mostly white, but there were brown gravy stains all over it. Some of the stains looked like they'd been there for a while. Others looked as though they'd just landed on the dress today.

As Katie reached up to wipe a bead of sweat from her cheek, she felt a sharp pain in her lower back—the kind her mother complained about when she'd spent too many hours standing up at work. Katie's feet really hurt, too. As she looked down, she was amazed to see just how huge her feet had become. Her white shoes looked like big boats on the ends of her legs!

"Excuse me," a fourth-grade boy said to Katie. "Can I have a hot dog and a carton of milk?"

That's when Katie realized what had happened to her.

Katie Carew had turned into Lucille the lunch lady!

Chapter 4

Now what? Katie thought nervously. *I can't do this. I don't want to touch that disgusting meat.*

"What's going on up there?" a sixth-grade girl shouted from the back of the line.

"The lunch lady is so slow," someone else said.

Katie felt like crying. She wasn't used to having kids yell at her. She didn't think being Lucille would be very much fun, but there was nothing she could do about it now.

Katie's only hope was that she had only been stuck inside Speedy's body for a little while. Maybe that's how it would work with

Lucille's body, too. Maybe the magic wind would change Katie back into herself pretty soon. She sure hoped so.

"Come on! Move it!" a sixth-grader shouted.

The kids were getting really mad. Katie wished she could just run away and hide, but there was nowhere for her to go. Katie had no choice. She was Lucille. She had to do what Lucille would do.

She had to serve disgusting food to kids.

"Oh man, not hot dogs again," a fifth-grade boy named Carlos moaned as he stared at a bucket of hot dogs swimming around in boiling water. "We had those yesterday, and three days before that."

"I know how you feel," Katie agreed. "I'm pretty sick of these hounds with Mississippi mud myself. Would you rather have a wimpy instead?"

Hounds with Mississippi mud? Wimpy? Katie was shocked as the weird words left her mouth. She'd never even heard those words before. But somehow she just seemed to know that a hound with Mississippi mud was a hot dog with mustard, and that a wimpy was a hamburger.

It must be some sort of lunchroom code that only lunch ladies know, Katie thought to herself.

"Who are you calling wimpy?" Carlos demanded in an angry voice.

Katie blushed. "Nobody. Wimpy means hamburger."

"Huh?" Carlos asked her.

"Oh, never mind." Katie replied in her best lunch lady voice. "Just move along."

A sixth-grade boy named Malcolm was next in line. "What's the sandwich today?" he asked her.

"Hen fruit," Katie answered. Oops! There was that lunchroom lingo again. "Uh, I mean egg salad," she explained quickly.

"Blech!" Malcolm exclaimed. "I hate egg salad."

Katie sighed. These kids were so mean. They were acting as though she'd cooked the food or something. She knew she had nothing to do with this menu. Lunch ladies weren't chefs. They just served what they were given. It wasn't like she was having a whole lot of fun serving the stuff, either. It was awful standing back there behind the counter, having to stare at rotting fruit and sniffing the scent of boiled hot dogs, overcooked baked beans, and egg salad all day long.

But Katie couldn't argue with Malcolm. She only had to *serve* the food. He actually had to eat it. Katie smiled at him and nodded her head. "I don't like egg salad very much, either," she said as she pointed to the egg salad tray. "Especially *this* egg salad. It's all gloppy. Too much mayonnaise."

"Like always," Malcolm moaned.

"You know where this egg salad belongs?" she asked Malcolm as she picked up a huge scooper full of the yellow-white glop.

"Where?" Malcolm said.

Katie gave him a naughty smile. "In the garbage!" she announced. Then she hurled the egg salad toward the garbage can.

Malcolm stared at her with surprise. He'd never seen Lucille the lunch lady throw food in the garbage before. Nobody had.

Katie watched as the big ball of egg salad soared in the direction of the trash can. Unfortunately, Katie's aim was not very good. The egg salad landed right on top of George's tray.

Katie gulped. *Maybe I should've worked on my throwing with Jeremy yesterday,* she thought to herself. Katie looked nervously at George. She couldn't tell if he was angry or not.

A big smile flashed across George's face. "*Food fight!*" he announced loudly. George shot a big glob of strawberry yogurt right at Kevin. The yogurt landed on a pile of tomato slices inside Kevin's lunch box.

Katie gasped. George shouldn't have done that. He knew how Kevin felt about tomatoes. Kevin was going to be really mad that George had ruined some of them!

A fifth-grader named Stanley was sitting at the next table. He began to laugh. "Looks like your lunch is gone," Stanley told Kevin. "You can't eat it now."

Kevin nodded. "I know. But there are lots of things you can do with a tomato!" He picked up a yogurt-covered tomato slice and flung it right at Stanley. The round slice land-ed in the middle of the fifth-grader's shirt. "Bulls-eye!" Kevin called out excitedly.

After that, it seemed like everyone in
the entire cafeteria started throwing food.
Stanley tossed his jelly sandwich toward the
table where class 3A was sitting. It landed
right on Jeremy's face. Suzanne began to giggle
as Jeremy wiped grape jelly from his glasses.
Jeremy threw a glob of mashed potatoes at
Suzanne. Suzanne rolled a piece of hot dog
bun into a little ball and threw it at Jeremy.

Mandy was so busy watching Suzanne and
Jeremy that she didn't notice a hot dog with
mustard flying towards her. It landed right
on her head. "Oooh! Gross!" she shouted out.
The hot dog slid onto the floor below, but the
mustard stayed in Mandy's hair.

Miriam started giggling. Mandy grinned
and shook her head wildly—splashing yellow
mustard all over Miriam.

Miriam picked up a slice of salami and
threw it at Mandy. Mandy ducked. The salami
landed on Zoe's nose.

George laughed so hard he fell off his

chair and landed on the floor. Zoe picked up her milk and poured it over George's head. George wiped the milk from his eyes, smiled, and licked his lips. "Mmmm!" he exclaimed. "Chocolate. My favorite!"

The kids were going wild! They launched lunchmeat. They flung frankfurters. They heaved hamburgers. Everyone and everything was covered with food. The teachers tried to stop the food fight, but they couldn't. The lunchroom was a mess.

Katie looked up. A canned peach was flying straight at her head. She ducked. The bright orange fruit smacked into the wall behind her and slid toward the floor.

"Look out!" Katie cried as she scooped up two huge handfuls of green Jell-O. "Here comes a Jell-O bomb!" She reached back and threw the glop across the room. The slimy Jell-O flew through the air and landed with a splat . . . *right in the middle of Mr. Kane's forehead.*

Katie had just slimed the school principal!

"Lucille!" Mr. Kane shouted in a very angry voice as he wiped the gooey green stuff from his eyes. "I'll see you in my office in fifteen minutes!"

The entire lunchroom froze. All eyes were on Katie.

Oh no! Katie had totally forgotten she was the lunch lady. She was in big trouble now. "Yes, sir," Katie told the principal, in Lucille's low, grown-up voice.

"As for you students," Mr. Kane continued, "you will be spending the rest of your day cleaning this cafeteria."

Chapter 5

As Katie walked down the hall, she felt a little sick. She had never been called down to the principal's office before—ever. Katie had never done anything bad in school in her whole life. *Until now.*

Katie knew Mr. Kane was going to give her a terrible punishment. She guessed it wasn't going to be something easy, like having to stay after school or writing a long apology note. This was going to be some sort of *grown-up* punishment. After all, Mr. Kane thought he was punishing Lucille the lunch lady, not Katie Carew from class 3A.

Suddenly Katie felt a gentle wind nip at

the back of her neck. She looked behind to see if someone had just opened a door or a window. No one was there.

Katie wasn't surprised when the calm wind began to get stronger. She wasn't shocked when it started blowing wildly around her like a tornado, either. She knew what was about to happen. Katie was going to change into someone else.

"Please, please, please let me turn back into me," she cried to the wind. "I just want to be Katie Carew. Nobody else."

The wind kept blowing harder and harder. Katie closed her eyes and held on tight to one of the lockers.

After a few minutes, the tornado stopped. The wind just disappeared, leaving no marks or traces in the hall. Not even one piece of paper was out of place. Slowly, Katie opened her eyes and looked down. Lucille's gravy-stained white dress was gone. Black jeans and a white sweater had taken its place. Those were the clothes Katie had worn to school that morning. Katie checked her reflection in a nearby classroom window. An eight-year-old girl with red hair, green eyes, and a line of

freckles on her nose looked back at her from the glass.

Katie Carew was back!

As Katie smiled at her reflection, she heard Mr. Kane's voice coming from his office.

"Lucille! I don't know what's gotten into you!" the principal yelled.

"I don't know what's gotten into me, either, Mr. Kane," Lucille said. "Come to think of it, I don't even know how I wound up here in your office."

Katie was surprised to hear the lunch lady's voice. How had she gotten to Mr. Kane's office so quickly? Did she know what had happened in the cafeteria? Did she remember that Katie had been inside her body?

"One minute, I'm in the cafeteria, handing out food. The next minute I'm standing here," Lucille continued. "I can't really remember anything in between."

"*Handing out food?*" Mr. Kane demanded. "Is that what you call slinging Jell-O across the cafeteria?"

"No sir," Lucille answered.

"Are you saying you *didn't* throw food in the cafeteria?" Mr. Kane asked her.

"No. I think I did throw food."

"You *think* you threw food?" Mr. Kane repeated.

Lucille shrugged. "I'm pretty sure I did . . . I think. I don't know. You saw me throw it, right?"

Mr. Kane nodded.

"So I must have," Lucille continued. "It's all very strange. I guess I just wasn't myself today."

"I can't understand what would make you waste perfectly good food," Mr. Kane continued.

"Well, I wouldn't call it 'perfectly good food,'" Lucille argued. "It's terrible food. We need to give those kids fresh fruits and vegetables, and there need to be more choices on the menu. I can understand why the kids treated the food like garbage. It *is* garbage. Now if I were in charge . . . "

That made Mr. Kane more angry than ever. "Well, you're not in charge," he told Lucille in a furious voice. "In fact, as of right now, you don't even work here anymore!"

Wow! Lucille had been fired! Now Katie felt really guilty. The food fight wasn't Lucille's fault. Katie wished she could run into Mr. Kane's office and tell him that it was her fault, but she knew the principal wouldn't believe her. A girl who turned into a lunch lady when a magical wind blew on her? Katie shook her head. Nobody would ever believe a story like that.

Quickly, Katie hurried back to the cafeteria. The least she could do was help the other kids clean up.

Chapter 6

That afternoon, Katie sat in her room with the door closed. She didn't feel very much like going out to play. Even if she did feel like playing, there'd be no one to play with. Most of the kids from school were grounded because they'd been in the food fight.

Still, Katie bet that none of the other kids felt as bad as she did. All they had lost was an afternoon of TV or a trip to the playground. Katie had made Lucille lose her job.

Katie began to cry. As soon as he saw Katie's tears, Pepper jumped up on the bed and sat beside her. He stuck out his big, red tongue and licked her face. But even a big, sloppy, wet, dog-kiss couldn't cheer up Katie. She used the back of her hand to wipe Pepper's slobber from her cheek. Pepper lifted his back paw and scratched at his floppy ear.

Just then there was a knock at the door. "Katie, Suzanne is on the phone," her mother said.

Katie walked downstairs to the kitchen and picked up the phone. "Hi, Suzanne," she said.

"Hey," Suzanne answered. "Where were you during the food fight today?"

"I . . . um . . . er . . . I was in the bathroom," Katie stammered. She hated lying to her friend, but she just couldn't tell her what had really happened.

"I can't believe you missed the whole thing," Suzanne continued. "It was amazing. Food was flying all over the place. I don't think I'll ever get the tomato juice off of my sweater. Kevin hit me in the back with a really squishy one!"

"Did it hurt?" Katie asked her.

"Nah," Suzanne said. "It was too mushy to hurt. It just sort of slid down my back. Besides, I got Kevin back—big time! I poured a container of grape juice over his head! His whole face turned purple. He looked like a space alien."

Katie giggled, a little.

"I don't think it's fair that Mrs. Derkman made you clean up with everyone else. You weren't even there." Suzanne continued. "It's such a bummer that you were in the bathroom! Katie, you always miss the good stuff."

"I heard all about it, though," Katie told Suzanne. "The whole school was talking about it when I got back to the cafeteria."

"But I'll bet you don't know what happened *after* the food fight," Suzanne said.

Katie smiled. Suzanne loved knowing things before anybody else did.

"What?" Katie asked her.

"Guess," Suzanne answered.

"Come on, Suzanne. Just tell me," Katie urged.

"Lucille the lunch lady got fired!" Suzanne exclaimed. "Mr. Kane told my mom when she came to pick me up. He said that he couldn't let a lunch lady who acted like an eight-year-old work in the school."

Katie felt guilty all over again.

"The weird thing was, Lucille *was* kinda acting like a kid," Suzanne continued. "I heard she told Malcolm the food belonged in the garbage. She even threw a bunch of it."

"That wasn't any reason to fire her," Katie interrupted her. "The food *is* really gross. We should have healthier stuff to eat."

"I guess," Suzanne agreed.

"And you know what else?" Katie continued. "Lucille didn't even really start the food fight. She was throwing some food out in the garbage and it landed on George by mistake. He started the food fight."

"How do you know that?" Suzanne asked her suddenly. "You weren't even there."

Oops! Katie had forgotten that she was supposed to have been in the girls room during the food fight. "Well, that's what I heard, anyway," she lied. "A bunch of kids said George was the one who yelled out 'food fight!' Maybe Mr. Kane should have fired him instead."

Suzanne laughed. "Mr. Kane can't fire a kid," she told Katie. "Kids have to go to school. It's a law."

"Well, anyway, it wasn't fair of Mr. Kane to fire Lucille," Katie continued.

"Oh who cares?" Suzanne said. "She's just a grouchy lunch lady. Besides, it was her own fault."

"She made a mistake," Katie insisted. "How'd you like it if you got punished every time you made a mistake? Everyone deserves a second chance—even grouches."

"I guess," Suzanne finally agreed. "But what can we do about it? We're just kids."

Katie was quiet for a minute, thinking. Suddenly an idea exploded in her head. "Suzanne, do you think you can bring a bag lunch for school tomorrow?" she asked excitedly.

"Sure, I guess so," Suzanne answered.

"Good. So will I," Katie said. "We have to call everyone we know and ask them to pack their lunches, too. Let's make sure every kid in the whole school brings a bag lunch tomorrow."

"I don't get it," Suzanne admitted. "How is that going to get Lucille her job back?"

"Nobody in our school is going to buy a cafeteria lunch until Lucille is back behind the counter!" Katie explained. "We're on a cafeteria strike!"

As soon as she hung up the phone with Suzanne, Katie called Jeremy and told him about the cafeteria strike. He had to let the boys know not to bring lunch money tomorrow.

"I don't know, Katie. Are you sure the kids will want to help Lucille?" Jeremy asked after Katie explained the plan to him. "She *is* kind of mean."

"Well, we're not so nice to her, either. All we ever do is complain about the food," Katie told him. "And she has a really hard job. It's hot back there in the kitchen. And she's standing up all the time. You wouldn't believe how badly her feet hurt!"

"How do you know that?" Jeremy asked.

Katie gulped. She'd almost let Jeremy know what had happened to her today. She needed to be more careful about what she said. "I . . . um . . . I'm just guessing that's how she feels," she stammered nervously. "Anyway, maybe Lucille would like us better if she knew we'd tried to get her job back for her."

"Maybe," Jeremy agreed. "She probably wouldn't have gotten fired if the food fight hadn't gotten wild. I guess it's kind of partly our fault."

"Exactly," Katie said. "That's why we should do this for her."

"It's worth a try, anyhow," Jeremy agreed. "What do you want me to do?"

"Just call two or three boys in our class and tell them about the strike," Katie instructed him. "Ask them to call a few of their friends. Then those kids can tell more kids, and they can tell more kids. If we keep the chain going all afternoon, by tomorrow everyone will know about the strike."

"I'll try," Jeremy assured Katie. "I hope it works."

"This plan has got to work," Katie answered. "It just has to!"

Chapter 7

The next morning, Katie had a lot of trouble sitting still in class. All she could think about was the cafeteria strike. Katie wasn't sure if all the kids in school had gotten phone calls. She wondered if everyone had agreed to bring their own lunches. If even one kid decided to buy lunch, the plan wouldn't work. They all had to stick together.

Luckily, as soon as she walked into the cafeteria, Katie knew she had nothing to worry about. No one was buying the school lunch. The cafeteria tables were covered with brown bags and lunch boxes the kids had brought from home.

Katie looked toward the counter. There was a new lunch lady standing there. She was short and chubby, with small gray eyes and big, yellow teeth. She looked *really* mean. She also looked really bored. None of the kids were buying lunch. The new lunch lady had nothing to do.

Katie smiled happily as she opened up her lunch bag.

"I thought you said your mom didn't have time to make you lunch in the morning," Suzanne remarked.

"She doesn't," Katie answered. "I made this myself." She took a big bite of her peanut butter and jelly sandwich. "It's pretty good. What do you have?"

Suzanne pulled a small plastic container from her brown bag. Inside the container were six evenly cut pieces of sushi. Suzanne took a pair of chopsticks from the bag and began to eat.

Katie glanced over at the next table where

the boys were sitting. Ever since Suzanne and Jeremy had argued over Speedy, the boys and girls in class 3A sat at separate tables. Katie felt bad about not being able to sit near Jeremy at lunch.

Of all the lunches in the cafeteria, George's was the most amazing. Most of the kids had brought lunch boxes or little brown bags with them to school. But not George. He was carrying a huge brown bag, the kind you got when you brought groceries home from the supermarket. Slowly, he began to empty the bag. First he unpacked a huge hero sandwich. Then he took out a pickle and a container of potato salad. Next he opened his Thermos and poured himself a cup of juice. Finally, he pulled a bag of corn chips out of the bag.

"Wow! That's some lunch!" Kevin exclaimed loud enough for Katie and the other girls to hear. "George, you are such a pig!"

George bit off a huge hunk of his hero and

began to snort. "Look at me, I'm a pig!" he shouted as he snorted.

"He's not kidding!" Suzanne said. "Only a pig would talk with his mouth full."

George leaned over toward the girls' table. He opened his mouth wide so Suzanne and Katie could see his half-chewed sandwich. "Hey, Katie Kazoo, check this out. I have seafood for lunch!" he told her. "Get it? *See* food?"

Katie giggled. George was definitely gross. He was also pretty funny.

"Speaking of pigs," George began as he swallowed his food. "What do you get when you mix a pig and an egg?"

"I don't know," Jeremy answered him. "What?"

"*Ham*pty Dumpty!" George exclaimed.

"Good one, George." Jeremy laughed. "I love your jokes."

"I've got a million of 'em!" George assured him. "What rescued Hampty Dumpty when he fell off the wall?"

"What?" Kevin asked.

"A *ham*bulance, of course," George replied. He chuckled really hard at his own joke.

Katie turned toward the food counter. The new lunch lady was still standing there. Her face looked a little sweaty now—probably because there was a lot of steam coming up from the food trays.

Just then, Mr. Kane walked into the cafeteria. The principal looked around the room. He stared at all the lunch boxes and brown paper bags on the tables. Then he headed toward the lunch line. Katie watched as Mr. Kane stared at all the uneaten food.

"What's going on in here?" Mr. Kane asked the new lunch lady.

"I don't know," she answered him. "Nobody's buying lunch."

Mr. Kane nodded his head slowly. Then he turned and faced the kids.

"Okay, kids, what's going on in here? Why isn't anyone buying lunch?" the principal asked.

" 'Cause we're on strike," a boy from the kindergarten called out. The grown-up words sounded funny coming from such a little boy. Everyone started to laugh, even Mr. Kane.

"You are?" Mr. Kane kneeled down next to him. "Why, Joshua?"

" 'Cause the lunch lady went away. We want her back," Josh explained.

Katie smiled as she watched the principal stand up and look around at all the brown bags and lunch boxes in the cafeteria. Now that he understood why the kids weren't buying lunches, Katie was sure the principal was going to tell them that Lucille could have her job back.

Katie sat up straight. She was about to be a hero.

But Katie was wrong. Mr. Kane didn't say a word. He just walked out of the room. Katie slumped down in her seat. This was not going to be as easy as she'd thought.

The students of Cherrydale Elementary School were not quitters. The next day they all brought their own lunches to school again. Once more, the new lunch lady stood all alone behind her trays. She looked even more angry, bored, and sweaty than she had the day before.

Katie took her seat next to Suzanne at the girls' table and opened her lunch bag.

"What do you have today?" Suzanne asked her.

"Peanut butter and jelly," Katie answered.

"Again?" Suzanne said.

Katie shrugged. "It's the only thing I know how to make. What have you got?"

"My mother gave me some leftover pizza with extra cheese," Suzanne said. "I like to eat it cold."

Katie glanced over toward the boys' table. Jeremy had brought a big bag of jelly beans to school. He was busy sharing them with Kevin and Carlos. Katie knew that if she were sitting over there, Jeremy would have let her have some of the purple ones. But the other boys didn't want Katie—or any of the girls—

sitting at their table.

Katie sure wished that Jeremy and Suzanne would stop fighting over the hamster. Their fight was ruining the whole class. Besides, they had to decide something fast. Tomorrow was Friday. Speedy still didn't have a home to go to for the weekend!

Katie also hoped that Mr. Kane would decide to hire Lucille back soon. The cafeteria was really starting to smell because of the strike. Since no one had bought the hot dogs yesterday, the lunch lady had brought them out again. School hot dogs always smelled pretty bad, but *day-old* school hot dogs really stank.

Just then, Mr. Kane walked toward the front of the cafeteria and looked out at the students. "It looks like we have a lot of uneaten food today, just like yesterday," he told them in a loud, stern voice. "I suppose it will be the same way tomorrow, too," he added.

Katie gulped. Mr. Kane sounded a little bit angry about the cafeteria strike. She was also pretty sure he was looking in her direction when he spoke. Did Mr. Kane know that Katie had started the cafeteria strike? Was he going to be angry with her? For the first time, Katie was worried about how the cafeteria strike was going to turn out.

But just then, Mr. Kane's stern frown turned upside down. He smiled at the children. "Well, I have good news for you kids," the principal said. "Lucille and I spoke on the phone today. I told her I thought she deserved a second chance."

Katie smiled. That's what she thought, too.

"You'll all be glad to know that Lucille said she'd come back to work . . . if you all promised to be good at lunch time," Mr. Kane told them.

"Hooray!" The kids in the cafeteria cheered.

"She also made me promise that we would have some better-tasting food and fresher vegetables. Starting tomorrow, we will have a different menu in the cafeteria."

"Hooray!" Once again, the kids began to shout wildly.

Mr. Kane looked sternly at the cheering kids. Everyone got quiet really quickly. "But

your food fight made a big mess of this room. We'll never get these walls completely cleaned up. You kids will have to stay after school for a few days to paint them."

Now the kids looked really sad. Painting the walls sounded like a boring job.

Just then, Katie had an idea. She raised her hand shyly. Mr. Kane looked over at her. "Yes, Katie," he said.

"Do we have to paint the walls this same color? Or can we paint a big picture on the wall instead?" she asked.

Mr. Kane thought about that for a minute. Then he nodded. "That's a wonderful idea, Katie. It would be nice to have a mural that was painted by our students." He smiled at the kids. "This cafeteria strike has proven that you can do great things when you all work together. I can't wait to see what kind of painting you can come up with."

"This is going to be the most beautiful cafeteria ever!" Katie assured the principal.

Chapter 8

The kids in class 3A began planning the mural as soon as Mr. Kane left the cafeteria.

"I think we should have unicorns and stars," Suzanne suggested.

"Oh yeah," Zoe agreed. "That sounds so pretty."

Kevin sat at the boys' table and rolled his eyes. "Would you listen to those girls? Who wants a *pretty* mural? I say we go for cool stuff like skateboards and hot-air balloons."

"Sounds good to me," Jeremy agreed.

"I'm not painting any dumb unicorn," George said.

That did it. Katie got up and stood right

between the two tables.

"Cut it out!" she shouted. "I'm tired of everybody fighting."

"It's her fault," Jeremy said, pointing at Suzanne.

"Are you nuts?" Suzanne shouted. "You started it."

"I don't care who started it," Katie said. "If we keep fighting we won't have any mural at all. We all have to work together."

"Okay, so what's it gonna be, Katie Kazoo? Skateboarders or unicorns?" George asked.

"I don't know," Katie admitted. "Maybe we could come up with something else. Something we're all happy with."

The kids thought about that for a minute.

"Okay," Suzanne agreed.

"You're right, Katie," Jeremy said quietly.

"So we're all friends again?" Katie asked nervously.

"I guess," Jeremy said. He looked across the aisle at Suzanne. "If we keep fighting over

Speedy, he won't have any place to go this weekend. Why don't you take him?"

Katie was surprised. She knew how badly Jeremy had wanted to take Speedy to his house.

Katie was even *more* surprised by Suzanne's answer.

"No, he's better off with you," Suzanne said. "Heather's stuff is pretty much all over my whole house. Everywhere you look there's a stroller or a changing table or a crib. I don't think there'd be any room for a hamster playground."

"But you know I have that big game on Saturday. I'm going to be busy with that," Jeremy told her.

Katie was worried all over again. Now it didn't sound like *either* of her friends wanted to take Speedy home. She had to do something fast!

"I have an idea," Katie said quickly. "Jeremy, you keep Speedy at your place.

Suzanne can come over on Saturday morning to give him his food and water while you're at the game."

"That's a good idea," Suzanne agreed. "Hey, and maybe on Sunday we could build him a hamster playground . . . together."

"Cool!" Jeremy exclaimed. "You know, my dad has a huge shoe box. It could be a cave."

"I'll bring over some paper towel rolls for Speedy to climb through," Suzanne said.

Katie sat quietly as she listened to Jeremy

 and Suzanne's plans for the hamster playground. She was really happy that her two best friends were getting along so well. She was also kind of sad. They were leaving her out of everything!

Jeremy guessed how Katie was feeling.

"Can you come over and help us build the playground?" he asked her.

Now Katie smiled brightly. "You bet!" she exclaimed.

Lunchtime was a whole lot more fun the next day. Katie stood on the lunch line right between her two best friends. It was nice not to have to choose between them any more.

When she reached the front of the line, Katie smiled brightly at Lucille. "I'll have a veggie wimpy and a cow juice," she told the lunch Lady. "And for dessert I'd like an Eve with a lid."

Lucille looked at Katie with surprise. She had no idea where the third grader had learned the secret lunchroom language, but she gave Katie a veggie burger, a container of milk, and a slice of apple pie anyway.

"Thanks," Katie told her. "It's good to have you back."

Lucille didn't say anything, but Katie thought she saw her smile a little.

As Katie followed Jeremy to a table near the back of the cafeteria, she felt a slight breeze blowing on the back of her neck. Katie looked around nervously. Was she about to change into someone else . . . right here in front of the whole school?

As Katie looked around, she noticed that the door to the playground was wide open. This was no magic wind. It was just a normal, everyday, outside kind of wind. Katie wasn't changing into anyone. She was staying Katie Kazoo.

At least for now.

Yummy Lunch Recipies!

Do you find the same old peanut-butter-and-jelly sandwiches in your lunch box every day? Are you sick of hard-boiled eggs and tuna salad? Well, here's the cure to the boring food blues. These easy-to-make lunch recipes are favorites of the kids in room 3A. Try them all. They're guaranteed to tickle your taste buds!

And after you've filled the inside of your lunch bag with these tasty treats, don't forget about the outside of the bag. Decorate your paper bag with stickers or funny pictures, just to make lunch time more special!

Cracker Stacker

You will need: round crackers, peanut butter, grape jelly.

Here's what you do: Start with a plain cracker. Spread peanut butter on the cracker. Put a second cracker on top of the first.

Spread jelly on the second cracker. Put a
third cracker on top of the second cracker.
Spread peanut butter on that one. Then top
that cracker with a fourth cracker. Spread
jelly on the top cracker. Keep going until you
have a stack of crackers. Wrap your cracker
stack in waxed paper before putting it in your
lunch box.

Banana Dogs

You will need: one banana, a hot dog roll,
peanut butter.

Here's what you do: Place the
banana in the hot dog roll. Smear the
banana with peanut butter just the
way you would smear mustard on a
hot dog. Wrap up your banana dog
in waxed paper and pack it in your lunch bag.

Inside-Out Sandwiches

You will need: one slice of bologna (use
soy bologna slices if you're a vegetarian like
Katie), one slice of American cheese, cream

cheese, peanut butter, two bread sticks.

Here's what you do: Lay out the slices of bologna and cheese. Spread cream cheese on one side of the balogna. Spread peanut butter on one side of the American cheese slice. Take one bread stick and wrap the meat around it. Make sure the cream cheese side is touching the bread stick. Wrap the American cheese slice around the second bread stick. Make sure the peanut butter side is touching the bread stick. Now you have two inside-out sandwiches. (The bread [stick]) is in the middle. Get it?) Place the sandwiches in a sealed sandwich bag and pack them in your lunch bag.

Shape-up Sandwiches

You will need: cream cheese, two slices of white or whole-wheat bread, raisins, grape jelly, cookie cutters.

Here's what you do: Spread cream cheese on one slice of bread. Sprinkle raisins on top of the cream cheese. Spread grape jelly on the other slice of bread. Place that slice on top of the raisins and cream cheese with the jelly-side-down. Use the cookie cutters to cut your sandwich into different shapes. Place your shaped sandwiches into plastic bags to keep them fresh.

A Gobble Gobble Good Sandwich

You will need: mayonnaise, three slices of white or whole wheat bread, two slices of turkey (or soy turkey), cranberry sauce, leftover stuffing.

Here's what you do: Spread a thin layer of mayonnaise on one slice of bread. Top the mayonnaise with turkey slices. Add the next slice of bread. Spread cranberry sauce on top of the bread. Place the stuffing on top of the cranberry sauce. Top with the last piece of bread. Store the sandwich in a plastic bag.

Katie Kazoo, SWITCHEROO

Oh, Baby!

Chapter 1

"So what did *you* do this weekend?" Jeremy Fox asked his best friend, Katie Carew. Katie, Jeremy, and Katie's *other* best friend, Suzanne Lock, were all standing in the schoolyard on Monday morning.

"I taught Pepper to roll over," Katie answered. Pepper was Katie's brown-and-white cocker spaniel.

"Can he do it?" Jeremy asked.

"Yeah. Pepper's real smart," Katie told him. "You just have to give him a treat and he'll do any trick."

"Maybe I should try that with Heather," Suzanne said. Heather was Suzanne's three-month-old sister. "She's been trying for days to roll over. She gets as far as her side and then she flops back down again."

Jeremy laughed. "I guess that means Katie's dog is smarter than your sister," he said.

Suzanne gave Jeremy a dirty look. Then she turned to Katie and smiled brightly. "I had the coolest weekend!" she said.

Katie choked back a giggle. Suzanne said the same thing every Monday morning. "What did you do?" she asked her.

"I went to the mall with my *dad*," Suzanne told her. "You know what *that* means."

"It means you got whatever you wanted," Jeremy said.

Suzanne nodded. "Exactly. That's how it always is with my dad. When he gets into a buying mood, he just shops, shops, shops!"

"My dad *never* gets in a buying mood," Katie sighed. "He hates shopping."

"Mine too," Jeremy agreed. "But I don't like to shop either, so it's okay."

"What did you get at the mall?" Katie asked Suzanne.

Suzanne pointed to her T-shirt. It was white with a big American flag in the middle. The stars were all made of glitter. "I got this shirt. I also got the new Bayside Boys CD. Its called *We're Back!*"

"You're so lucky!" Katie exclaimed. "That CD just came out. I'll bet you're the first one in school to get it."

Suzanne smiled broadly. "Gee, you think so?"

"So, is it any good?" Jeremy asked her.

"Oh yeah!" Suzanne exclaimed. "Even better than the *first* Bayside Boys CD. I was dancing around my room all day yesterday."

Jeremy nodded "I heard the new song on the radio. They're a pretty good group," he agreed.

Suzanne stared at him with surprise. "*Pretty* good?" she demanded. "They're not pretty good. They're the best!"

"I don't know about that," Jeremy said.

"Well, I do," Suzanne argued. "They're the

greatest group in the whole world. Don't you think so, Katie?"

Katie twirled a lock of her red hair around her finger nervously. She hated it when her two best friends disagreed. It always left her stuck in the middle. No matter what she said, someone would be mad.

"I like them a lot," Katie told Suzanne finally. "At least, I liked their first CD. I haven't heard this one yet."

"It's great," Suzanne assured her. "I think everyone should get it. In fact . . ." Suzanne stopped in the middle of her sentence and smiled at Jeremy. "Are all of the articles for this week's *3A Times* written yet? she asked.

Jeremy was the editor of the *3A Times*, the class newspaper. He was the one who asked people to write articles.

"Not yet," Jeremy told Suzanne.

"Good! Suzanne declared. "I want to write about the new Bayside Boys CD. I want to tell everyone how great it is."

Jeremy pulled a small black notebook from his bag. He pushed his wire glasses up on his nose and looked at a list of articles. "Okay," he told Suzanne finally. "I have room for one more story."

"Great!" Suzanne exclaimed. "I'll get started tonight."

As Jeremy put away his notebook, their teacher, Mrs. Derkman, blew a loud whistle. "Class 3A, line up," she called out across the playground.

Chapter 2

"Hey there, Katie Kazoo," George Brennan said as he walked past her into the classroom.

Katie smiled. Katie Kazoo was the nickname George had given her. When he had first started calling her that, it made her kind of mad. But now she liked being Katie Kazoo. It sounded cool.

"Hi, George," she said.

"So do you know what the rug said to the floor?" George asked Katie.

Katie laughed. That would have seemed like a weird question from anyone else. But Katie knew it was just of one of George's jokes. George *loved* to tell jokes.

"No, what *did* the rug say to the floor?" Katie asked.

"I've got you covered!" George exclaimed. He laughed at his own joke. Katie laughed too.

"If you liked that one, you'll love this one," George continued. "What did one cucumber say to the other cucumber?"

"What?" Katie said.

"If you'd kept your mouth shut, we wouldn't be in this pickle," George told her.

Katie giggled harder. "That one was *really* funny."

"Katie, please find your seat," Mrs. Derkman interrupted.

Katie blushed. Quickly, she scrambled to her desk.

George began to head over toward his desk, too, but Mrs. Derkman blocked his path. "You don't need to sit down, George," Mrs. Derkman said.

"I don't?" George asked.

Mrs. Derkman shook her head. "Since

you're so interested in speaking during class, you can go to the front of the room and give your current-events report."

Usually, George hated when it was his turn to talk about current events. But today he grinned as he pulled a newspaper article from his binder.

"My article is about the movie *Tornado*," he told the class.

Before he could say another word, Mrs. Derkman interrupted him. "That's not really current events, George," she said.

George looked very sad—so sad that Mrs. Derkman said, "Well, why don't you tell us about it anyway?"

George smiled brightly. "*Tornado* just opened this weekend," he began. "It earned almost seventy-five million dollars in ticket sales. That's a lot of money. A lot of people think that it could be the biggest-selling movie of all time. They think it could win a lot of awards, too. All those people are right.

Tornado is a great movie. I should know. I saw it with Kevin on Saturday."

Wow!

Everyone stared at George and Kevin. It was hard to believe they had been brave enough to go see *Tornado*. The ads on TV looked really scary.

"Any questions?" George asked. You were always supposed to ask for questions at the end of your current-events report.

"Was the movie as scary as it looks on TV?" Mandy Banks asked.

"Scarier," George said proudly.

"Did your parents take you to see it?" Miriam Chan wondered.

"Nope, Kevin's big brother, Ian, took us," George said.

"Did you sit through the whole thing?" Manny Gonzalez asked.

"Of course," George told him.

"Did the tornado look real?" Jeremy asked.

"Totally!" George nodded.

Just then, Mrs. Derkman stood up and
walked to the front of the room. "Thank you
for that report," she told George. "If any of
you have more questions for George or Kevin,
you can ask them at lunch. Right now, please
take out your math workbooks."

Katie was glad that Mrs. Derkman had changed the subject. Katie didn't like scary movies. She was especially afraid of big winds, like the kind they showed in *Tornado*. There was a good reason for that. Katie had been swept up in big winds herself. *Twice.*

And both times her life had really changed.

It had all started on a day when Katie was so sad that she'd wished she could be anyone but herself. There must have been a shooting star in the sky at the time, because Katie's wish came true. The next thing she knew, a big, strong, magic wind was blowing all around her. When the wind stopped, Katie had been turned into Speedy, the class hamster!

Katie changed back into herself pretty fast, but the magic wind wasn't through with her. A couple of days later it blew again . . . turning Katie into Lucille, the lunch lady in the cafeteria. Talk about *awful*. She'd had to serve disgusting cafeteria food!

It had been a few weeks since that last disaster. But Katie was convinced the magic wind would be back. She just didn't know when. And she didn't know who it would turn her into.

That was scarier than any movie could ever be!

Chapter 3

At lunchtime, everyone tried to sit near Kevin and George. They wanted to hear all about *Tornado*.

"This house gets lifted right up in the air," Kevin said. "And it didn't look fake like that tiny house in *The Wizard of Oz*. It was a real flying house." He took a big bite of his tomato. Tomatoes were Kevin's favorite food.

"I doubt it was a real house," Suzanne argued. "It was probably just some dumb special effect."

"How would you know, Suzanne?" Kevin asked her. "You haven't seen *Tornado*."

Suzanne rolled her eyes. She looked across

the table at where Miriam and Mandy were sitting. "Do you guys want to come over after school to hear the new Bayside Boys CD?" she asked. "I just got it."

Mandy shook her head. "Thanks anyway, but my older sister bought that CD on Friday. She and her friends were playing it all weekend long."

"My brother got it, too," Miriam added. "I probably heard it thirty times yesterday."

Mandy moved closer to George. "Were you scared at the part of the movie when the tornado came near the mall?" she asked him. Suzanne didn't wait for George's answer. She stood up and walked away from the table. Jeremy followed behind her.

"Um, Suzanne, I wanted to talk to you about that Bayside Boys article you were going to write," he said slowly.

"What about it?" Suzanne asked.

"Well, it's just that it seems like everyone has heard the CD already. There's no real

reason to put an article about it in the newspaper," Jeremy told her. "I'm going to ask George and Kevin to write an article about *Tornado* instead."

Suzanne turned away and stormed over to where Katie was sitting. "We need to talk," Suzanne said.

Katie nodded. She took the last bite of her sandwich, then followed Suzanne to the girls' room. Suzanne looked under all the stalls to make sure no one was there. No one was. They were alone.

"We have to see *Tornado*," Suzanne said finally.

"Why?" Katie asked.

"Because George and Kevin have seen it," Suzanne explained.

"So what?" Katie asked.

Suzanne's face was getting red. "We can't let those boys do something we haven't done."

"My mother would never let me see *Tornado*," Katie said.

"Well, you could ask her, couldn't you?" Suzanne begged. "Katie, I *have* to see that movie. And I can't go alone."

Katie sighed. She really didn't want to see *Tornado*, but it seemed so important to Suzanne. She didn't want to let her friend down. Still, she didn't want to be scared, either. No matter what she did, Katie was going to be unhappy.

So why should Suzanne be unhappy, too?

"Okay," Katie said finally. "I'll ask my mom."

Chapter 4

"Katie, I just don't think *Tornado* is a movie you should see. You'll get nightmares," Katie's mom explained while she and Katie were sitting in the kitchen having milk and cookies after school.

Katie took a bite of her cookie. "Okay," she said. She chomped down on a chocolate chip. Katie's mother looked at her daughter strangely. She thought Katie would argue with her. But Katie didn't say anything. After all, she didn't really want to see the movie. At least now she could tell Suzanne that she'd tried.

"Can I go over to Suzanne's?" Katie asked.

Her mother nodded. "Be back for supper."

As Katie went outside, Pepper followed close behind. Together they headed down the block toward Suzanne's house.

"Hey, wait up!"

Katie turned around to see Jeremy coming toward her. "What are you doing?" Jeremy asked her.

"I was just going to Suzanne's," Katie said. "Wanna come?"

Jeremy shook his head slowly. "She probably wouldn't want to see me."

"She would if you said you were sorry," Katie told him.

"I guess it wasn't very nice of me to replace her newspaper story with George and Kevin's," Jeremy admitted.

Katie shook her head.

"Maybe I'll come with you and apologize," Jeremy suggested.

Katie smiled. "Good idea," she said.

Suzanne was sitting on her front porch when Katie, Pepper, and Jeremy arrived. She scowled when she saw Jeremy.

"Why is he here?" she asked Katie.

"He wants to apologize," Katie told her.

"I'm sorry, Suzanne," Jeremy said. "It wasn't fair of me to take your article away. I should have made George and Kevin wait until next week. I won't do it again."

Suzanne shrugged and held out her little finger. "Pinky swear?"

Jeremy crooked his finger through hers. "Pinky swear."

But Suzanne still looked sad.

"*Now* what's wrong?" Katie asked her.

"My mother said I couldn't go to see
Tornado," Suzanne said. "She said I'm too

young. I am *so* sick of being treated like a baby around here. I'm supposed to be the big one. *Heather's* the baby!"

"*Wah! Wah!*" Just then, baby Heather started crying.

"I have to go see what's wrong," Suzanne said as she stood up. "My mom's doing the laundry," she explained. "I'm supposed to take care of Heather until she's finished."

Wow! Suzanne was in charge. Katie was very impressed.

The crying was even louder inside. "What's wrong with her?" Katie asked as she looked down into the playpen. Heather's face was red and covered with tears.

"Maybe she's hungry," Suzanne guessed. "I've got to get her bottle and a baby bib."

"I'll get the bottle," Katie volunteered.

Suzanne shook her head. "Pepper follows you everywhere. If he gets dirty paw-prints on the kitchen floor, my mom will have a fit. She just mopped it."

"So *I'll* get the bottle," Jeremy said.

"Okay," Suzanne said. "It's in the refrigerator. I've got to go upstairs and get her bib."

"*Wah! Wah!*"

Katie was alone with the screaming baby. She covered her ears. Pepper let out a little howl.

Just then, Katie felt a strange wind blow against the back of her neck. She looked towards the front door. Maybe they'd left it open when they'd come inside.

But the door was closed. So were the windows.

Oh, no!

This was no ordinary wind. This was the magic wind. And it was getting stronger.

Katie looked over toward Pepper. She wanted to make sure he was safe. But the wind didn't seem to be blowing anywhere near the dog. He was just standing there watching Katie.

Katie was really scared. The wind was big,

powerful, and out of control. But Katie grew even *more* afraid when the wind *stopped* blowing. She knew what that meant.

The magic wind was gone . . . and so was Katie Carew.

Chapter 5

"RUFF! RUFF! RUFF!"

Pepper's bark rang through the house. It sounded so deep and loud. *That's weird,* Katie thought to herself. *Pepper's never barked like that before.*

"Where am I?" she wondered. "*Who* am I?" Wherever she was, she was lying down. There were thick wooden bars all around her. Katie could see Pepper's face staring at her through the bars. The rest of the room seemed blurry. *Something's wrong with my eyes*, she thought. Katie's ears were working just fine, though. She could hear Pepper loud and clear.

"AROOO!" Pepper howled.

Too loud and clear!

Katie's nose was working well, too. Something nearby really stunk. It smelled like the school bathroom at the end of day.

Blech! Katie had to get away from that smell. Quickly, she struggled to stand up. But she couldn't seem to climb to her feet. She tried to sit up, but her body wouldn't bend the right way.

Katie couldn't stand. She couldn't sit. She couldn't even roll over to see where she was. All she could do was lie there staring up at the blurry ceiling.

Then, suddenly, something caught Katie's eye. A mobile made of black-and-white animals hung right over her head. Katie watched as the tiny puppies and kittens traveled around and around. It was kind of fun to see them face her and then turn away again.

As she stared at the animals, Katie began to suck on one of her fingers. It calmed her down—until she realized she wasn't sucking on her finger at all. She was sucking on her big toe. *Yuck!*

The bathroom smell was getting really gross. Watching the animals go around was making her dizzy. Pepper's barking was giving her a headache. And now her whole mouth tasted like feet!

It was all too awful. Katie burst into tears.

Suzanne stormed into the room. "Katie, you have to make Pepper stop barking," she said. Then she stopped and looked around. "Katie, where are you?"

Suzanne couldn't see her! Now Katie was really scared. *What if the magic wind made me invisible this time?* she thought.

"Come on, Katie. I know you're here. Quit fooling around," Suzanne called out again.

Katie was afraid to answer her. If Suzanne heard a voice coming from an invisible girl, she'd be really scared. Katie didn't want to scare her friend.

Just then, Jeremy walked into the room. "I've got the bottle," he said.

"Thanks," Suzanne replied. "Have you seen Katie?"

Jeremy shrugged. "No. But she couldn't have gone far. Pepper's still here."

"That's true." Suzanne agreed.

"Maybe she's in the bathroom," Jeremy said.

Suzanne shrugged. "Maybe. Anyhow, I've got to feed Heather. She's crying again. Pepper's barking is making her nuts."

Suddenly Katie felt something or someone grab her and lift her off the ground. Katie looked down. The floor seemed very far away. Katie couldn't help it. She started crying all over again.

"Don't cry," Katie heard Suzanne say.

Katie looked up to find a giant Suzanne-head

staring down at her. Her mouth seemed *huge*.

"Here you go," Suzanne said as she shoved a big blob of rubber into Katie's mouth. A sweet, smelly liquid poured out onto Katie's tongue.

"Isn't that yummy, Heather?" Suzanne asked.

Heather?

Katie's eyes grew wide with fear. The magic wind hadn't made her invisible. It had turned her into Suzanne's baby sister!

"*WAH!*"

Chapter 6

"I don't get it," Jeremy said. "I thought that bottle was supposed to make her stop crying."

"So did I," Suzanne agreed. She pulled the bottle from Katie's mouth. "Maybe she's not hungry." Katie wanted to explain to her friends that she wasn't crying because she was hungry. She was crying because she didn't want to be stuck in Heather's tiny body.

But Katie knew she couldn't say anything. She was supposed to be a baby! Babies didn't talk. Suzanne and Jeremy would totally flip out if they knew who this baby really was.

"Let me try one more time," Suzanne said. She shoved the bottle back into Katie's mouth.

Katie made a face and tried to spit the bottle out. But Suzanne held it tight. Katie had no choice. Slowly she began to suck at the smelly, sweet baby formula. As she sucked, she glanced at the clock on the wall. It said 4:45.

Oh, no! Katie's mother had warned her to be home in time for dinner. If the magic wind didn't change her back soon, Katie would be eating baby formula for dinner. And baby formula tasted awful. Katie squirmed and tried to spit the stuff out of her mouth.

"Nope, she's definitely not hungry," Suzanne said finally.

"Then why is she still crying?" Jeremy asked.

"I think she's wet," Suzanne told him. "So what does that mean?"

Suzanne rolled her eyes. "It means we have to change her diaper," she told him.

Jeremy shook his head wildly. "No way!" he declared. "*We* don't have to change her diaper. *You* have to change her diaper. I'm not going near that thing."

190

"Fine, I'll do it," Suzanne said. She picked up the baby and carried her to the table.

Oh, no! Katie thought nervously. Her best friend was about to change her diaper. There was no way that was going to happen!

Katie was so upset, she completely forgot that she was a baby. She opened her mouth and began to scream.

"No, don't!" Katie cried out. She kicked her legs wildly. "Stop!"

Suzanne jumped back with surprise. She looked over at Jeremy. "What did you say?" she asked him.

"I didn't say anything," Jeremy replied. "I thought you did."

"I didn't say anything, either," Suzanne told him.

Jeremy looked at her curiously. "If you didn't say anything, and I didn't say anything, who said that?"

"Stop kidding around," Suzanne told him. "Let me just change the baby and then . . ."

But Katie wasn't going to let that happen. "I said *don't*!" she shouted out again. "I'm fine, guys. There's no wet diaper here. I'm just crying. You know how us babies can be."

Suzanne and Jeremy stared at the baby with amazement.

"Did you hear that?" Suzanne asked Jeremy.

"Uh-huh," Jeremy said slowly.

"Heather talked," Suzanne shouted. "She definitely talked."

"Uh huh," Jeremy said again. He couldn't seem to say anything else.

"But she's only three months old," Suzanne said. "Three-month-old babies can't talk. Unless . . ."

"Unless what?" Jeremy asked her.

"Unless she's a genius!" Suzanne declared. "Heather is the smartest baby in the world!" Suzanne picked the baby up and put her into the playpen. "You stay here," she told Jeremy. "I've got to get my mom!"

As soon as Suzanne was out of the room, Jeremy headed for the front door. He let it slam behind him as he left.

Katie wondered what was so important that Jeremy had to leave right away. But she was glad to be by herself for a few minutes. Well, sort of by herself. Pepper was still in the room with her. The dog walked over to the playpen and stared at Katie.

"I sure hope I turn back into me soon," Katie told her dog. "I can't put off this diaper change thing forever. She squirmed uncomfortably. "I really do think I'm wet in here!"

Pepper barked softly. He knew what it felt like to have an accident.

Just then, Katie felt a familiar breeze begin to blow around Heather's playpen. Katie knew right away that it wasn't an ordinary wind. By now, she could feel the difference between the magic wind and just plain wind. She closed her eyes tight. Katie knew what was going to happen now.

The wind began to blow stronger. The small playpen rocked back and forth wildly. As the wind circled around her, Katie got really scared. The wind was very strong, and she was very small. What if the wind carried her right out of the playpen? Where would she wind up?

Katie gulped. She knew she would never get used to the magic wind. Oh *why* had she ever wished to be anyone other than herself? Right now, she really wished she could be Katie Carew again.

She wanted to be wearing her own clothes—including her dry underpants.

She wanted to be tall enough to look in a mirror and see her own red hair and green eyes.

Katie licked a drip of sticky baby formula from her lip. She wouldn't mind being home in time for dinner, either.

Chapter 7

"Is this ever going to end?" Katie screamed out as the magic wind circled around her. By now the wind was so strong and loud that she was sure no one could hear her. Katie began to cry as if she *were* a real baby. This was the worst the magic wind had ever been.

And then it stopped—just as suddenly as it had begun. Everything in the room was completely still.

Katie blinked as her eyes focused on a bright white light. It took a minute for her to realize that the light was coming from the ceiling in Suzanne's living room. That was where she'd been before the wind had blown.

And she was still lying flat on her back.

Hadn't the wind changed anything? Was she still baby Heather?

Nervously, Katie looked down toward her feet. Instead of ten tiny toes, Katie saw her bright, red platform sneakers.

"I wouldn't want to put *those* in my mouth," Katie laughed to herself.

Then she looked at her hands. Her fingers were the regular size. The chipped blue nail polish she had forgotten to take off was still there.

No doubt about it. Katie was herself again!

Pepper came over and licked Katie's face. "You knew who I was the whole time, didn't you, boy?" she said as she reached over to pet him. "You're such a smart dog." Pepper licked her face again.

Just then, Katie heard Suzanne's voice. "Honest, Mom, Heather talked to us. She told Jeremy and me not to change her diaper!" Suzanne exclaimed. She practically tripped over Katie as she came into the room.

"Watch it!" Katie called out.

"What are you doing down there?" Suzanne asked her best friend.

"Oh, just lying around," Katie answered nervously as she jumped to her feet. She smiled. It felt good to be standing again.

"Where's Jeremy?" Suzanne asked her.

"I don't know. I guess he left," Katie told her. "He was gone by the time I got back from the bathroom."

Of course, Katie had never actually left

the room. She felt bad about lying to Suzanne, but there was no way Katie could tell her the truth. Suzanne would never believe it anyway.

"Well, you really missed it," Suzanne told Katie. "It was amazing. Heather talked. And not just *goo goo gaa* stuff. She *really* talked."

"Suzanne, I need to get back to the laundry," her mother said. "So if you're finished with this nonsense . . ."

"It's not nonsense," Suzanne insisted. She walked over to the playpen. "I'll bet she'll do it again." Suzanne looked down at her baby sister. "Heather, do you want me to change your diaper?"

Baby Heather stared up at her big sister. She didn't make a sound.

"Come on, Heather," Suzanne urged again. "Are you wet?"

This time, Heather opened her mouth wide.

"Look! She's going to say something!" Suzanne exclaimed.

"WAHHHHHHHH!!!!" Heather let out the

loudest cry Katie had ever heard.

"Well, there's your answer," Suzanne's mother said as she left the room. "She's wet, and she needs her diaper changed."

Suzanne looked like she was about to cry, too. She turned to Katie. "She really did talk," Suzanne insisted. "She *is* the smartest baby ever!"

Katie handed Suzanne a diaper. "I think Heather's really smart . . . even if she doesn't

say another word until she's one year old,"
she said.

"But that's when *every* baby talks,"
Suzanne said. "Heather's special."

Katie smiled. "Of course she is," she said
kindly. "Just look at who she has for a sister."

Chapter 8

By the time Katie and Suzanne got to school the next morning, a whole crowd of kids had gathered on the playground. George was the first one to spot the girls coming toward them.

"Hey, Katie Kazoo! Suzanne! Look at this!" he called out. He waved a sheet of white paper high in the air.

"What's that?" Katie asked him.

"The *3A Times*," George told her. "Check it out."

"No, thanks," Suzanne told him. "I've heard enough about *Tornado*."

"Oh, we never wrote that article," George told her. "We forgot."

"Figures," Suzanne said.

"So then what's in the newspaper?" Katie asked George.

"Look!"

Katie took the newspaper from George's hand. Right there, on the front page, was a huge headline. It read:

SUZANNE'S SISTER SPEAKS!
Genius baby learns to talk!

Suzanne grinned. "Now, this is what I call news," she said.

Jeremy walked over toward the girls and George. "I wrote the article yesterday after I left your house," he told Suzanne.

Miriam and Mandy raced over to Suzanne.

"What did Heather say, exactly?" Miriam asked.

"Did she really tell you not to change her diaper?" Mandy added.

"Yes!" Suzanne smiled. She really liked all the attention she was getting. "I always knew my sister would be smart, but I never thought she'd be a genius!"

Katie watched as Suzanne talked to the crowd of kids gathered around her. She looked very happy.

"Hey, do you guys know why a mother carries her baby?" George asked the others.

"Why?" Manny asked him.

"Because a baby can't carry her mother!" George answered.

A few of the kids giggled. But most of the class was too busy listening to Suzanne to laugh at George's joke.

Katie could see that George was kind of sad that the kids hadn't thought his joke was really funny. She felt bad for him.

"I liked that one," she whispered to George.

"I can always count on you, Katie Kazoo," George rhymed. "Have you heard this one? Why do moms dress baby girls in pink and baby boys in blue?"

"Why?" Katie asked.

"Because babies can't dress themselves."

Katie giggled. "Very funny."

Just then Mrs. Derkman blew her whistle. It was time to go inside. As the kids lined up, Katie heard Suzanne still talking about Heather.

"Why don't you guys come by after school?" Suzanne said. "Then you can hear Heather for yourselves."

Katie gulped. "Suzanne," she whispered nervously. "I'm not sure that's a good idea."

"Why not?" Suzanne asked.

"Well, you never know. What if Heather doesn't feel like talking again?" Katie said.

"Don't you believe Heather talked?" Kevin asked Katie.

Katie blushed. "Um sure, I guess I do," she said nervously. "But . . ."

"You didn't hear her yesterday," Suzanne told Katie. "I think you're just jealous that you missed it." Suzanne rolled her eyes at Katie. "Can I help it if you're never around when the good stuff happens?"

That made Katie mad! She wasn't jealous at all. She was just trying to keep Suzanne from being embarrassed. Well, if her friend was going act like that, let her bring the other kids home. She'd see.

Chapter 9

That afternoon, a whole crowd of third graders followed Suzanne home from school. They weren't just kids from Class 3A, either. By the time the end of the day rolled around, almost everyone in the grade had heard about the amazing talking baby.

"You know, I think we should make a videotape of Heather talking," Suzanne told Jeremy as they walked toward Suzanne's house. "She could be on the news."

Jeremy nodded. "She could be famous."

Suzanne looked at the crowd of third graders trailing behind her. "I think she already is."

George and Katie were walking toward the back of the group. "Suzanne seems really happy," George told Katie.

"I guess," Katie said glumly. She knew Suzanne wouldn't be very glad for long.

George studied Katie's frown. "I know how to make you laugh, Katie Kazoo."

George walked over toward Miriam Chan. He opened his mouth wide and pushed on one of his top teeth with his tongue. The tooth wiggled all the way around in a circle. It was really loose.

Miriam made a face. "Eeww! George, that's gross!" she shouted. "Close your mouth."

Katie giggled. Everything grossed Miriam out.

"See, I told you I could make you laugh." George said.

But Katie's laughter didn't last for long. As soon as they reached Suzanne's house, she had that old guilty feeling again. If only she'd told Suzanne about the magic wind, none of this would be happening. But Katie knew she couldn't do that. She couldn't tell anyone.

"You guys wait here," Suzanne said as she went into her house. "I'll bring Heather out."

A moment later, Suzanne came outside again, holding Heather in her arms. "Okay, Heather," Suzanne said. "Say hello to my friends."

Heather looked up at her big sister. "A-goo," she said quietly.

"That's baby talk," Kevin shouted out. "Any baby can do that."

Suzanne shook her head. "She's just warming up," she insisted. "Go ahead, Heather. Say something."

"A-goo," Heather repeated.

"There's nothing special about that baby," Andrew Epstein from Class 3B said, as he and some of his friends left.

"She can't talk," Kevin declared. "Suzanne, you're such a liar."

"I am not!" Suzanne insisted. She looked at Jeremy. "Tell them, Jeremy!"

Jeremy nodded. "She really can talk, you guys. I heard her."

Kevin frowned. "Next time, save it for April Fools' Day."

"Yeah, you should leave the joking to the experts," George added.

"It's no joke," Jeremy insisted. "I wouldn't have written about a joke in the *3A Times*."

"You shouldn't have put this in the paper," Manny said as he walked away. "Mrs. Derkman is going to be so mad!"

Jeremy gulped. If the kids didn't believe them, Mrs. Derkman probably wouldn't, either. He was going to be in big trouble.

Before long, Suzanne, Jeremy, and Katie

were the only ones left standing outside the house. Suzanne looked angrily at Katie. "I'll bet this makes you really happy," she told her.

Katie was really hurt. She never wanted Suzanne and Jeremy to be embarrassed. "No, it doesn't," she insisted.

But Suzanne was too upset to hear her. She took Heather into the house.

Jeremy turned to Katie. "Katie, you believe us, don't you?" he asked. "It had to have been Heather talking. No one else was in the room. Where else could that voice have come from? The bookshelf?"

Jeremy was being silly. But what he said gave Katie a great idea. She knew how to prove that her friends weren't lying—without having to to tell anyone about the magic wind.

"Sorry, Jeremy, I gotta go," Katie said. She raced off down the block.

"Some best friend you are!" Jeremy groaned angrily as he watched her run.

Chapter 10

The minute she got home, Katie darted upstairs to her room. "Don't you want a snack?" her mother called after her.

"No, thanks," Katie shouted back. "I've got too much to do."

Katie spent the rest of the afternoon in her room working on her plan to save Jeremy and Suzanne. She didn't even want to take the time to eat dinner, but her mother made her.

"You must have an awful lot of homework," Katie's mother said as she piled stir-fried tofu and broccoli onto Katie's plate. Katie's mom and dad were both having meat-loaf, but Katie was a vegetarian. She had decided a few months ago that she was never, ever going to eat anything that had had a face.

Katie shrugged and shoveled her food into her mouth. She chewed as fast as she could. "There! All done," Katie said, showing her parents her empty plate. "May I be excused?"

Katie's mother looked surprised. Usually Katie had to be forced to finish her broccoli. (Just because she was a vegetarian didn't mean she loved *every* vegetable!)

"It was very good," Katie assured her mom.

"I'm glad. I guess you can be excused."

"Thanks!" Katie yelled as she ran back up the stairs toward her room.

"This plan had better work," she said to Pepper as she flopped down and opened the big book on her bed. "It's the only chance Suzanne and Jeremy have."

The next morning, as Katie arrived at school, she saw Suzanne and Jeremy standing by themselves on the blacktop. Suzanne was

kicking angrily at the ground. Jeremy kept fiddling with his glasses.

A bunch of other kids were standing by a tree, pointing at Jeremy and Suzanne. Katie walked right past her two best friends, and joined the group of giggling third graders.

"Man, those two are such jerks!" Kevin declared.

"Yeah, they were just jealous that you got to see *Tornado*," Mandy told him.

"They're big liars," Miriam added.

"Maybe they're not lying," Katie interrupted.

All the other kids stared at her.

"Give me a break," Manny declared. "Just because they're your best friends doesn't mean you have to take their side, Katie. Heather can't talk."

"I know," Katie agreed. "But that doesn't mean they didn't hear her say something."

Manny looked around. "Huh?" he asked. "That's impossible."

"Wanna bet, wise guy?"

Manny looked around some more. "Who said that?" he demanded.

"I did."

"Who said *that*?" Manny repeated.

"*Hello*! Down here!"

George looked down. "I think it's coming from your backpack," he said.

"Yeah, right," Manny said. He turned to see if anyone was standing behind him.

"Don't turn your back on me," the voice said. "I want to see your face for a change.

That made George laugh. "Hey, that's pretty good. Get it? A backpack *always* faces your back!"

Now Manny was confused. "Backpacks can't talk," he insisted. But he stared down toward his pack anyway.

"It sure sounds like your backpack was talking to you, Manny," Katie said.

"That's impossible," Manny declared. "There's no one in there."

"Come see," the voice said. "Take a peek inside!"

Now Manny was getting nervous. So were the other kids.

"Go check the backpack," Katie said sweetly.

"Not me," Manny replied in a small, scared voice.

"Why?" Katie asked him. "Are you chicken?"

Manny didn't answer.

"I'll check it," George said bravely. "Come on, Kevin."

Kevin shook his head. "Leave me out of this," he said. "That backpack's haunted or something."

Katie started to laugh. "You guys are such babies," she said.

She bent down and unzipped the pack. George stood beside her and looked inside.

"Nothing in here but your lunch and your math worksheet," he assured Manny. "Ooh. I think you got number five completely wrong!"

Manny blushed. "See, I told you there was no one in there," he said.

"But the the backpack was talking, right?" Katie asked Manny. "You heard it."

Manny nodded slowly.

"Or at least you *thought* you heard it," Katie added. "Just like Jeremy and Suzanne thought they heard Heather talk."

"This is different," Manny said. "I really did hear the backpack talk. We all did."

Katie started to laugh. "Nope. You heard me talk," she said. "That's *my* voice."

"No way," Kevin told her. "You weren't talking."

"Yes, I was," Katie insisted. "I was talking without moving my lips. I made it *seem* like the voice was coming from the backpack. But it was really coming from me."

"Wow!" George exclaimed.

"It's called ventriloquism," Katie continued. "I played the same trick on Jeremy and Suzanne. It wasn't Heather talking. It was me."

Katie bit her lip. That wasn't a *complete* lie. She really was talking for Heather that afternoon. Of course, that's because she had *been* Heather.

"Wow!" George exclaimed. "That's so cool. How did you learn to to do that?"

"My mother bought me a book on ventriloquism for Christmas last year. I've been practicing forever to get it right."

"Can you do some more?" Miriam asked. Katie smiled. "Sure."

For the next few minutes Katie made Mandy's math notebook whisper, George's sneaker sing, and Miriam's pocketbook cry.

"I guess we owe Jeremy and Suzanne an apology," Kevin admitted. Katie watched from far away as the other kids went over to talk to Suzanne and Jeremy. Suzanne glanced over at Katie angrily. Jeremy was so mad he wouldn't even look in her direction.

Katie was suddenly very glad she'd learned ventriloquism. It seemed like she was going to be spending a lot of time talking to herself.

Chapter 11

At lunchtime, Katie sat all by herself in the back of the cafeteria. But Suzanne found her anyway. She came storming over with a really angry look on her face.

"I can't believe you did that to us!" Suzanne shouted at Katie.

"I'm sorry," Katie apologized. "But I did warn you not to bring everyone to hear Heather talk."

"Oh, I'm not mad about that," Suzanne told her. "I'm totally over it. All the kids know I wasn't lying."

Katie looked surprised. "You're really over it?"

"Sure. But I'm still mad at you."

"Why?" Katie asked.

"I thought we were best friends. We're supposed to tell each other everything."

Katie gulped. Had Suzanne found out her secret? Did she know about the magic wind?

"How come you didn't tell me you were a ventriloquist?" Suzanne demanded. "We could have been playing tricks on people all this time."

Katie smiled. *What a relief.* Suzanne didn't know about the wind after all. "I practiced my ventriloquism all last night. I wanted it to be perfect today," Katie told her.

"It worked," Suzanne told her. "Everyone was totally impressed."

"Then you're really not upset with me?" Katie asked.

Suzanne shrugged. "Nah. I guess it was a pretty funny joke. Besides, you're the one who had to go tell Mrs. Derkman that you fooled Jeremy into writing a fake article for the *3A Times.*"

"That *was* pretty awful," Katie admitted. "Mrs. Derkman was really angry."

"What's your punishment?" Suzanne asked.

"She's making me write a one-page report about some old ventriloquist named Edgar Bergen."

Suzanne wrinkled her nose. "Extra homework!" she declared. "That's *really* bad."

Just then, Jeremy walked over. "Hey, guys," he said as he put down his tray. He looked curiously at Katie. "How come you're sitting all the way over here?"

Katie blushed and stared at the floor. "I figured you'd be mad at me," she said.

Jeremy nodded. "I was. But I'll forgive you . . . if you do something for me."

"Anything," Katie told him.

"Teach me how to be a ventriloquist. I know a few people I want to play tricks on!" Jeremy said.

Katie grinned. "It's a deal."

"I can't believe I didn't know you could do that," Jeremy said.

Katie thought about all the times the magic wind had turned her into someone else: Speedy the hamster. Lucille the lunch lady. Baby Heather.

"I guess there are a lot of things you guys don't know about me," she admitted finally.

"Like what?" Suzanne asked.

Katie grinned. "That's for me to know and for you to find out!" she teased. Then she looked down at Jeremy's sandwich.

"Aren't you gonna eat me?" the sandwich seemed to say.

"Hey, that's really good!" Jeremy admitted. "Show me how you did that."

As Katie gave her two friends their first ventriloquism lesson, she felt happy inside. It was nice to have things back to normal again.

Talk Like Katie!

At least for a little while.

Here are some of the ventriloquism tricks that Katie taught Jeremy and Suzanne. Practice them at home. Then see if you can fool your friends!

It's easy to say these letters without moving your lips: A, C, D, E, G, H, I, J, K, L, N, O, Q, R, S, T, U, X, Y, Z. But most words have other sounds in them, too. Like the letter B—you can't say *that* without moving your lips, can you?

So just how do ventriloquists say words like "banana" or "bubble"? Here's their secret: instead of making a B sound, they use a D sound. The trick is to quickly slur over the D sound so it sounds sort of like a B.

229

These are some other ventriloquist tricks:

*To say a word with a P sound, use a T sound instead.

*If you want to say the letter F, make a TH sound, like the one you hear in "thanks."

*If you need to make a V sound, say TH like in the word "there."

*To make a W sound, try using an OO sound, like in the word "boot."

Just remember, it will take a while before the words sound right. It takes a lot of practice to learn to talk without moving your lips. Try to practice in front of a mirror. That way you can see how well you're doing.

When you're ready, try putting on a ventriloquist show! Any puppet will do—even a sock puppet. (Just wash the sock first. Nobody wants a sock puppet that smells like feet!)

If you're making your puppet speak, be sure to look right at him. That way it will seem like the puppet is talking, not you. If you make your puppet tell a joke, be sure to laugh when the audience does. After all, the joke was funny, wasn't it?

Here are some of George Brennan's favorite jokes. You can use them in your act, or you can make up a few of your own.

What cat can't you trust?
A cheetah!

What's the difference between the North Pole and the South Pole?
The whole world!

What's the difference between here and there?
The letter T!

Why did the rooster run away from the fight?
Because he was chicken!

Why do hummingbirds hum?
Because they don't know the words!

Katie Kazoo, SWITCHEROO

Girls Don't Have Cooties

Chapter 1

"Here comes Jeremy," Suzanne Lock said. She looked out across the school playground. She quickly handed her best friend Katie Carew an envelope. "Put this in your backpack, fast!"

Katie looked at the envelope curiously. "What's the big secret?" she asked.

"It's an invitation to a party, this Saturday, at my house," Suzanne quickly explained.

"Oh," Katie answered. "So why do I have to hide it from Jeremy? Just give him his invitation too."

Suzanne shook her head. "Jeremy's not invited. No boys are. It's just for the *girls* in our class."

Katie was shocked. "You mean you're only asking half of our friends to your party? You can't do that. We've been friends with Jeremy forever."

Suzanne shook her head. "Jeremy's *your* best friend, Katie, not mine," she insisted. "I only hang out with him when you're around."

Katie couldn't argue with that. It was true. Jeremy Fox and Suzanne were both Katie's best friends. The two of them got along okay when they were with Katie. But Jeremy and Suzanne didn't always like each other.

"What kind of party is it?" Katie asked.

"A sleepover!" Suzanne told her excitedly. "I'm going to rent some movies. We'll do each other's hair and play games. My mom even said we can put on makeup—if we wash it off before we go to sleep." Suzanne flashed Katie a secret smile. "Of course, we're not going to sleep at all. Who sleeps at a sleepover?"

Katie shrugged. She didn't know how to

answer that. She'd never been to a sleepover party before.

"So, will you come?" Suzanne asked her.

Katie nodded. "Sure. Sounds like fun."

"Hey you guys! What's up?" Jeremy asked as he walked over to where Suzanne and Katie were standing.

Katie quickly stuffed her invitation into her backpack. "Um, *nothing*," Katie murmured. She

suddenly felt a little guilty about Suzanne's all-girl party—even though she wasn't the one who was throwing it.

"I gotta go," Suzanne said quickly. "I need to talk to Mandy and Miriam about something important." She winked at Katie. Katie looked away.

Jeremy laughed as Suzanne walked off. "Suzanne's so funny," he said.

"Why?" Katie asked.

"She's always got something important to tell someone," he said. "Doesn't she ever have *nothing* to say?"

Katie giggled. "Not Suzanne. Even if she did, she'd make a big deal about how she had nothing to say."

Jeremy nodded. Then he changed the subject. "My parents are taking me to the Magic Lamp Amusement Park on Saturday night. We're going to check out that new Lightning Bolt roller coaster. They said I could bring a friend. Wanna come?"

Katie's eyes flashed. The Lightning Bolt was supposed to be an amazing roller coaster. The TV commercials said it has three loops and goes really fast!

"Wow! The Lightning Bolt would be a great one to add to my list!" she exclaimed. Katie was trying to go on at least fifty roller coasters before she became a grown-up. So far she'd been on seven different ones.

"That's what I thought," Jeremy told her.

"I would love to go . . ." Katie began. Then she remembered Suzanne's party. "Except I can't go Saturday night," she finished sadly.

"How come?" Jeremy asked her.

"Well . . . um . . . I . . .er . . ." Katie stammered nervously. "I kind of promised to hang out with Suzanne on Saturday night," she said finally.

That was the truth. Jeremy didn't have to know about the all-girl party.

Jeremy thought about that for a minute. "I guess I can bring two friends."

Katie gulped. She really didn't want to have to tell Jeremy about Suzanne's party. It would only hurt his feelings.

"Suzanne doesn't like roller coasters much," Katie said quickly.

"That's okay. Neither does my mom. They could go on the bumper cars while we're on the Lightning Bolt."

Katie sighed. "Well . . . see . . . Suzanne and I sort of have plans with some of the other girls in the class on Saturday night and . . ."

"What kind of plans?" Jeremy interrupted her.

"It's nothing you'd want to do," Katie insisted.

"What are you doing?" Jeremy asked again.

"Well, Suzanne's having this all-girl party," Katie blurted out finally.

Jeremy pushed his glasses up on his nose and stared at Katie. He looked angry. "How come she's only inviting girls?" he asked.

"That's not nice."

"It's a sleepover party," Katie explained. "We're going to put on makeup and do our hair and stuff. You wouldn't want to do that."

"It's still not fair!"

"But Jeremy, it's a *sleepover*!" Katie insisted again. "Boys *can't* come."

Jeremy didn't want to hear it. "Suzanne is being a total snob. She should have a party everyone can come to." He stormed away angrily.

"Where are you going?" Katie called after him.

"I'm going to talk to George and Manny," Jeremy told her. "Wait until *they* hear about this. They're going to be mad!"

Katie played nervously with a lock of her red hair as she watched Jeremy walk away. She had a feeling this was not going to be a good day in class 3A.

Chapter 2

By lunchtime, Jeremy had told all the boys in class 3A about Suzanne's sleepover party. Katie could tell they were mad because they were all sitting together at half of the lunch table. They were also giving the girls really dirty looks.

The girls were sitting at the other end of the table. They were giving the boys dirty looks right back.

By the time Katie reached the lunch table, the only seat left was next to George Brennan and Zoe Canter—right between the girls and the boys. She put her tray down and slid onto her chair.

George jumped up and moved his chair away from Katie. He picked up his hand and made believe he was holding some sort of spray can.

"We want all girls to go away. Blast them hard with cootie spray!" He pretended to spritz Katie all over with invisible spray. "*Pffft*," he said, imitating a spray can.

Katie jumped up with surprise. "George? What are you doing?"

George shrugged. "I'm sorry, Katie Kazoo. But you're a girl. All girls have cooties. I'm

just making sure I don't get them from you."

"What are you talking about?" she asked George.

George moved his chair even farther from Katie. "Oooh! Get this girl away from me!" he shouted. All the boys laughed.

That made Katie upset. George was her friend. He was the one who had given her the nickname Katie Kazoo. They told jokes together and played after school. Katie was the very first kid to become George's friend when he was the new kid at school. Now he wouldn't even sit next to her.

"Come on, George, cut it out!" Katie insisted.

George didn't answer. Instead he took a huge bite of his bologna sandwich and turned toward his buddy, Kevin Camilleri.

"Aachoo!" George let out a really fake sneeze. Pieces of chewed-up bologna, cheese, and bread, sprayed out of his mouth and all over the table.

Kevin chuckled. "Good one, George!"

"Eeeeew! Yuck!" Miriam Chan shouted. She was sitting across from Katie. That gave her a clear view of George's flying food.

"Boys are really gross," Miriam's best friend Mandy Banks said.

"I don't know how you can be friends with any of them, Katie."

Katie sighed. She hated it when there were fights between the boys and the girls.

Just a few weeks ago, Suzanne and Jeremy had had a fight about who would get to take Speedy, the class hamster, home for the weekend. The whole class had gotten involved in that war. The boys had sided with Jeremy, and the girls had sided with Suzanne. Katie had been stuck in the middle—right between her two best friends.

Katie sighed. "I wish this didn't always . . ." Katie was about to wish that this didn't always have to happen to her, but she stopped herself. She'd learned the hard way to be really careful about what she wished for.

It had all started one rotten day. Katie had
ruined her favorite jeans, lost the football game
for her team, and belched really loudly in front
of the whole class. That day, Katie had wished
that she could be anyone but herself.

Right after that, the magic wind came.

The magic wind was big and horrible, like
a tornado. But it only stormed around Katie.
Nobody else could see it or feel it. Whenever
the magic wind came, it turned Katie into
someone else.

The first time the wind had come, it
changed Katie into Speedy, the class hamster! She'd spent a whole morning nibbling on
chew sticks and running on a hamster wheel.

Luckily, Katie changed back into herself
pretty fast. *Un*luckily, the magic wind had
come back again. It turned Katie into Lucille,
the cafeteria lunch lady.

But serving mystery meat to her friends
wasn't nearly as bad as the next time the
wind came. That time it turned Katie into

Suzanne's baby sister, Heather. Katie had come *this* close to having her best friend change her diaper. How embarrassing would *that* have been?

So Katie didn't make wishes anymore. She never knew what would happen if they came true.

Just then, George and Kevin snuck up behind Miriam and Mandy.

"*Pffft!*" the boys shouted. "We want all girls to go away. Blast them hard with cootie spray."

"Get away!" Mandy cried out. "*You're* the ones with cooties."

"No way," George argued. "Girls have cooties."

Katie looked across the table at Jeremy. He was sitting next to Manny Gonzalez. When he saw Katie staring at him, Jeremy looked down at the floor. But Manny didn't look away. He smiled and held up an imaginary spray can. *Pffft.* He pretended to spritz Katie with cootie spray.

Katie was getting mad. *Really mad.*

"*Girls don't have cooties!*" she shouted.
Then she jumped up and ran out of the
cafeteria.

Chapter 3

"Hey Katie, where are you going?" Suzanne asked as she ran after her best friend.

"I can't stand this fighting anymore!" Katie told her.

"Then stop hanging around with the boys," Suzanne suggested. "They started it all."

Katie wanted to tell Suzanne that that wasn't true. Suzanne had actually started it all by having an all-girl party. But Katie already had one best friend refusing to talk to her. She couldn't take it if Suzanne ignored her, too.

"Katie, come on outside," Suzanne said.

"We're going to play double Dutch jump rope. Mandy and Zoe have already said that they'll be steady enders."

That was good. Mandy and Zoe were the only ones who knew how to turn both double Dutch jump ropes at the same time without getting them tangled.

"Okay," Katie agreed. "Just let me run back to the classroom and get my jean jacket."

"Great! I'll see ya out on the playground!" Suzanne said with a grin.

The classroom was empty. Katie ran in, grabbed her jacket, and headed straight for the door.

But before she could leave the room, she felt a strange breeze tingle against the back of her neck. Katie put on her jacket, and raised the collar around her neck. But she could still feel the breeze blowing.

She looked around the room. The windows

248

were all shut. The breeze was obviously not coming from outside.

"Oh no!" Katie cried out. "Not again."

The magic wind was back. And she knew there was nothing she could do to stop it.

The wind began to circle strongly around Katie. Her red hair whipped wildly around her head. The tornado swirled faster and faster. Katie held on to a desk so she wouldn't blow away. She closed her eyes tightly, and tried not to cry.

It seemed like the wind was blowing for a very long time. But it was probably just a few seconds before it stopped, just as suddenly as it had begun.

Katie knew what that meant. She wasn't Katie Carew anymore. She was someone else.

The question was, who was she?

Chapter 4

Before Katie opened her eyes, she sniffed at the air around her. The smells had changed. Room 3A smelled like a mix of chalk dust, crayons, and Speedy's hamster litter. *This* room smelled like food—tuna sandwiches, ketchup, french fries, and milk.

Oh, no! This had to be the cafeteria. Had Katie become Lucille the Lunch Lady . . . again?

Slowly, Katie opened her eyes. At first everything looked blurry. Then Katie reached up to her nose and slid her glasses back up toward her eyes.

Glasses? Wait a minute. Katie didn't wear glasses. Who was she?

Katie looked down at her clothes. She was wearing a pair of jeans, black sneakers, and a denim jacket. Typical third-grade clothes.

Okay, so she was a kid. But *which* kid?

Before Katie could figure that out, Kevin poured his chocolate milk onto what was left of his tuna hero. "Hey check this out," he said. "Pretty gross, huh?"

George shook his head. "That's nothing," he said. "Watch this!" He mixed tuna salad into his chocolate pudding and stirred it with ketchup-covered french fries. "Now that's what I call gross!"

Katie looked down at the mess George had just made. It was brown and red, with bits of gray tuna and mayonnaise floating in it. It was possibly the most disgusting thing she'd ever seen.

"See, I told you this was super-colossal-gross," George bragged. "Jeremy looks like he's about to puke just from looking at it."

"I dare you to eat that," Kevin said to George.

That was too much for Katie. If George swallowed a spoonful of that mess she was going to be sick. "No, don't!" she cried out.

George looked over toward Katie. "Relax, Jeremy," he said. "Even I wouldn't eat that mess!"

Jeremy?

Oh, no! Was it possible the magic wind had turned her into her own best friend? Her *boy* best friend?

Of course it was possible. The magic wind could do anything.

"You ready, Captain?" George asked Katie suddenly.

Katie looked back at him. "Ready for what?" she asked, confused.

"The soccer game, remember? You're one of the captains."

"Huh?" Katie asked. "I am?"

"Sure you are," George said. "You're always captain. You're our best player."

"I'm the other captain," bragged Andrew Epstein from class 3B.

"You are?" Katie asked him.

Andrew looked a little annoyed. "We decided this morning, remember?"

"You ready, Jeremy?" Kevin asked Katie. "I want to get out to the field before recess is over."

"Yeah, sure," Katie mumbled nervously. "I think we should go to the bathroom before the game," George suggested. "No time-outs for pee breaks."

"Good idea," Kevin agreed. "Besides, I like the boys' room. No cootie-carrying girls are allowed in there."

Katie gulped. Kevin was right. Not about the cooties, of course. He was only right about girls not being allowed in the boys' room. Boys weren't allowed in the girls' room, either.

Katie wasn't quite sure *which* bathroom she belonged in anymore. After all, she was only Jeremy on the outside. She was still Katie on the inside. The thought of going into the boys bathroom was absolutely, *positively* gross!

Good thing Katie didn't actually *have* to go.

"Not me," Katie said quickly. "You know me, I can hold it forever. I'm like a camel!"

George shrugged. "So you go get the soccer ball. We'll meet you on the field."

Phew! That was close!

Katie had gotten out of that one. But she was pretty sure things weren't going to be that easy once they were out on the field. Katie wasn't a very good soccer player. Her only hope was that Jeremy's body would know what to do once she started playing.

Or, better yet, maybe the magic wind would change her back before the soccer game began.

Chapter 5

"Hey, that took you long enough," Kevin said as he and George caught up to Katie on her way to the soccer field.

Katie was walking very slowly. She was in no hurry to get onto that field.

"Pick me first, Jeremy," George pleaded. "I want to be on your team. Andrew's team never wins."

"Yeah," Kevin agreed. "Andrew and his friends play like girls."

"So what?" Katie asked. "Some girls are great at soccer."

George laughed. "That was funny, Jeremy," he said. "I didn't know you liked to tell jokes."

"I'm not kidding," Katie said.

"Yeah, right," Kevin answered. "Could you just see us playing against the girls? They'd probably want a time-out to fix their hair."

"Or because they broke a nail," George added. He made his voice sound high and squeaky. "Time out for a nail-polish emergency!" he joked.

Katie watched as Kevin and George laughed. They were making her really mad.

Then, suddenly Katie got an idea. *Let them laugh,* she thought to herself. *I'll show them!*

×　　×　　×

"Okay, let's choose up teams," Andrew said, once all the boys were on the soccer field. "Okay if I go first, Jeremy?"

Katie nodded.

"I choose Kevin," Andrew said.

"Oh, man!" Kevin moaned as he moved over next to Andrew.

"I choose George," Katie said.

"Yes!" George cheered. He gave Katie a high-five.

"Now I'll take Billy," Andrew told them.

Katie looked at the crowd of boys standing in front of her. They all wanted to be on Jeremy's team. Slowly she turned to face the playground—where the girls were.

"Hey Mandy!" she called out. "You want to play soccer?"

Suddenly, everything stopped. The girls dropped their jump ropes. The boys stared in surprise.

"Jeremy, what are you doing?" George asked.

"I'm choosing up teams," Katie told him.

"But you can't pick Mandy," George said.

"Why not?"

George looked amazed. "Because she's a girl!"

Katie sighed. "Yeah. But she's also a really good soccer player. Maybe the best in the class. She could win the game for us."

"Sure," George moaned. "We'd win because the other team would be laughing too hard to play!"

"I still choose Mandy," Katie told him.

"I'm not playing with her," George said. "I'm going over to Andrew's team."

"Andrew's team is the *only* team," Kevin said. "No one wants to play with a girl."

"Except Jeremy," Andrew pointed out.

"Jeremy the *girl lover*!" George shouted.

"Girl lover, girl lover!" The other boys began chanting. "Jeremy's a girl lover!"

Kevin lifted his hand and sprayed some imaginary cootie spray. We want all girl *lovers* to go away. Blast them hard with cootie spray!" he shouted.

"Let's get out of here, you guys!" George told the others. "We don't want to get cooties from Jeremy the girl lover!"

The boys ran over to the playground.

"Get 'em!" George shouted, as he ran straight toward Suzanne and blasted her with imaginary cootie spray.

Katie stood alone on the soccer field and watched the boys chase the girls. She'd wanted to fix things between the girls and the boys. That's why she'd picked Mandy for Jeremy's team.

"I hate you, George!" Suzanne cried out.

Katie sighed. Instead things were worse than ever.

Chapter 6

It was lonely on the soccer field. All the other kids were running around on the playground. They didn't even notice that one of their friends was standing there, all alone.

These days, the worst thing any boy in 3A could be called was a girl lover! Katie knew that when Jeremy found out what had happened, he was going to be upset. And it was all Katie's fault.

Usually, when the magic wind turned Katie into someone else, she couldn't wait to become Katie Carew again. But this time was diferent. Katie didn't want to turn back into herself. She wanted to stay Jeremy for a little longer. At least long enough to fix things.

But the magic wind never seemed to care what Katie wanted. Suddenly, a cool breeze began to blow. Katie looked over toward the trees. The leaves were still. She glanced over at the flag post. The flag wasn't moving. *The magic wind was back.*

Once again, wild winds began to circle around Katie. The magic wind was so strong that it whipped off Jeremy's glasses. Katie reached out to grab them, but the glasses flew across the field.

Oh, no! Jeremy wouldn't be able to see without his glasses. Katie tried to run after them. The magic wind wouldn't let her move. It was holding her prisoner.

And then it just stopped. Slowly Katie opened her eyes. She looked around. She was still out on the soccer field.

Okay, so now she knew where she was. But she still didn't know who she was.

Nervously, Katie looked down at her feet.

There were her purple shoes and her pink glitter pants.

She held up her hands. She was still wearing the same electric green, glow-in-the-dark nail polish she'd put on the day before.

Katie was back.

And so was Jeremy Fox. He was standing just a few feet from Katie on the field. Jeremy looked kind of funny without his glasses on. Katie hardly ever saw him like that.

"Where am I?" Jeremy mumbled to himself. He squinted his eyes and tried to find his glasses.

Katie spotted Jeremy's glasses by a tree. She picked them up and handed them to him. "Looking for these?" she asked him.

"What happened?" Jeremy asked. "I mean, I sort of remember coming out here, but . . ."

Katie gulped. How was she going to explain what happened? She couldn't just say that the magic wind had turned her into Jeremy. He'd never believe her. If it hadn't

happened to her, Katie wouldn't believe it, either.

"What do you mean you 'sort of remember'?" Katie asked him.

Before Jeremy could answer, George's teasing voice rang out over the playground. "Hey! Look at the girl lover talking to Katie Kazoo!"

Jeremy's face turned beet red.

"Jeremy's a girl lover! Jeremy's a girl

lover!" the boys all began to chant.

Jeremy's put his glasses on and stared at the boys angrily.

"Who are you calling a girl lover?" he asked them.

"You!" Kevin shouted back.

"Who says?" Jeremy asked.

"Hey, you're the one who picked a girl for your soccer team!" Manny told him.

Jeremy looked confused. "What are you talking about?"

"Hello? Aren't you the one who picked Mandy Banks to be on your team?" George asked.

Jeremy thought for a minute. "I think I remember something like that," he began. "I don't know. It's all kind of weird."

"We thought it was pretty weird too," Manny told him.

"*Scary* weird," Andrew added.

"Next thing you know, you'll be putting on a frilly nightgown and going to Suzanne's dumb old sleepover party," George said. He pretended to hold up the edges of an invisible skirt.

Just the mention of Suzanne's party made Jeremy really mad. There was no way he was going to be called a girl lover!

"Hey, can't you guys take a joke?" Jeremy asked.

"Huh?" Kevin asked.

"It was just a joke," Jeremy told them. "Come on, George. You love jokes. You must have known I was kidding. I would never play soccer with a girl!"

George thought about that. "I don't know, Jeremy. You seemed pretty serious out there."

"I'm not a girl lover!" Jeremy insisted.

Katie couldn't believe her ears. How could Jeremy say that? They had been best friends since they were babies.

Jeremy looked away from Katie's sad, angry eyes. "I wouldn't be caught dead near a girl!" he assured the boys.

"Oh yeah?" Manny asked. "Prove it!"

Jeremy thought about that for a minute. Then he got an idea. "Okay, you guys meet me by the slide after school. Those girls think it's okay to have a party without us? We'll show them!"

Just then, Mrs. Derkman blew her loud whistle. "Class 3A line up!" she called out. "Recess is over."

As the boys raced to line up, George whispered to Jeremy, "This had better be good!"

"Oh it is," Jeremy assured him. "It's *really* good!"

Chapter 7

After school, Katie and Suzanne went to Katie's house. "What do you think the boys are planning?" Katie asked Suzanne as the girls walked into Katie's bedroom.

"Who knows?" Suzanne answered, plopping down on the bed. "Who *cares*? No matter what they're planning, it won't be as fun as my sleepover party."

Just then Pepper, Katie's cocker spaniel, padded into the room. He hopped up on the bed and licked Katie's face.

"I guess Pepper is the only boy who'll hang out with me anymore." Katie kissed her dog right on his cold, wet nose.

"Blech!" Suzanne exclaimed. "I don't know how you can kiss Pepper. He's got dog breath!"

"It's not so bad," Katie told her.

"I guess not," Suzanne agreed. "It can't be any worse than George Brennan's breath after he eats pickles and Doritos."

Katie laughed. George did eat some weird food combinations. "No, it's definitely not *that* bad. I don't mind kissing Pepper. He's like part of my family."

"Exactly," Suzanne said. "He's not like a human boy. He'd never turn on you the way Jeremy did!"

Katie frowned. She wished Suzanne hadn't brought that up. Jeremy had hurt Katie's feelings—big time.

"Where were you today during recess, anyway?" Suzanne asked Katie suddenly. "You went to get your jacket and then you just disappeared."

Katie didn't say anything. There was no way she could explain what had happened to her.

"Well, you definitely missed it," Suzanne continued. "Nobody could believe it when Jeremy picked Mandy to be on his team. It was really mean of him to tease her like that."

"Are you sure he was teasing?" Katie asked.

"Of course. The boys would never have let her play," Suzanne said.

"But Mandy is a good player," Katie replied.

"I know," Suzanne agreed. "The boys are *afraid* to play against her."

Katie shrugged. "I guess."

Suzanne smiled and pulled a notebook from her backpack. "I don't want to waste one more minute talking about those yucky boys," she said. "I want to plan my sleepover party. It's going to be the best ever!"

Katie listened as Suzanne talked on and on about junk food, movies, and flashlight games. It wasn't all that interesting, but it was better than thinking about what the boys

were planning. There was going to be real
trouble in school tomorrow, and Katie couldn't
help but feel that it was all her fault.

Chapter 8

By the time Katie got to school the next morning, all of the boys in class 3A were already there. They'd gathered under a tree.

Katie walked over to the crowd of boys. "Hey Jeremy, what's going on?" she asked her pal.

Jeremy turned away and didn't answer.

"Come on, Jeremy, cut it out," Katie said. "Answer me."

"Go away Katie," he told her. "You can't be here."

"Why not?" she said.

"Because this is a meeting of the Boys Club," Kevin butted in. *"No girls allowed!"*

"What Boys Club?" Katie asked.

"It's our new club," Manny told her. "We have a club handshake and a club language. They're secret. Only boys can know them."

"Oh, come on guys, we can tell Katie Kazoo," George said suddenly.

"Are you nuts?" Kevin asked him.

"Nah. Katie's cool. We can teach *her* our secret language," George said.

Katie was surprised. She was also happy. Maybe this fighting was finally going to end.

"Yeah, I'm cool," she assured the boys.

"So, repeat after me," George told her. "*Awa.*"

"*Awa,*" Katie repeated.

"*Ta si.*"

"*Ta si.*"

"*Lee goo.*"

"*Lee goo.*"

"*Siam,*" George finished.

"*Siam,*" Katie said.

George nodded. "Good. Now put it all together."

Katie took a deep breath. "Okay, here goes. *Awa ta si lee goo siam,*" she said. All the boys started to laugh.

At first Katie didn't know what was so funny. Then she figured it out. When she said the words all together, it sounded like "Oh what a silly goose I am!"

"Gotcha!" George told her. "We'll *never* reveal our secrets to a girl. Now get out of here!"

Katie choked back the tears as she walked away.

"What's wrong?" Suzanne said when she spotted Katie walking alone on the playground.

"The boys have started a club," Katie told her.

"So what?" Suzanne asked.

"No girls are allowed," Katie explained.

"Like I said, *so what?*" Suzanne said. "We should start our own club. A Girls Club. It'll be so much better than theirs."

Just then, the boys started chanting their new cheer. "Girls go to Jupiter to get more stupider. Boys go to college to get more knowledge!" the boys shouted.

"Oh, please!" Suzanne said. "That is so old. The last time I heard that one I fell off my dinosaur."

Katie didn't laugh. Her feelings were too hurt.

Suzanne smiled and put her arm around Katie. "Come on. Let's get the other girls," she said. "I know we can come up with something better than that!"

Chapter 9

By lunchtime, the all-new Girls Club had its own cheer. "Shout it big! Shout it proud! We're the girls club. No boys allowed. Stomp your feet. Make some noise. Let everyone know. *We hate boys!*" they chanted.

Then the boys started to shout their cheer. "Girls go to Jupiter to get more stupider. Boys go to college to get more knowledge!" They made sure they cheered even louder than the girls.

Soon, both clubs were screaming their cheers. The whole cafeteria heard them. Unfortunately, so did Mrs. Derkman. She blew her whistle loudly.

Everyone stopped screaming. It was the first time Mrs. Derkman had ever blown her whistle *inside*. She must have been really angry!

"That's enough!" the teacher shouted. "There will be no recess after lunch. I want you all to sit here and think about how you are acting."

"That's not fair!" George shouted. "The girls started it!"

Suzanne opened her mouth to argue. Then she saw the look on Mrs. Derkman's face. She closed her mouth.

A few minutes later, class 3A was alone in the cafeteria. Everyone else was playing outside.

"This is so unfair," Mandy moaned. She put her head down on the table.

"If they hadn't started that dumb Boys Club, none of this would have happened," Miriam agreed.

"I wish we could get them back for everything they've done," Zoe added.

Suzanne grinned. "I know how we can," she said. She whispered something to Mandy.

"Great idea!" Mandy agreed.

"What? What?" Zoe asked.

The girls all gathered around Suzanne. All the girls *except* Katie, that is. Katie didn't want to hear Suzanne's latest idea. She knew it would be a mean idea. There had been enough meanness in class 3A already.

For a while all the girls were quiet. They were waiting for Mrs. Derkman to leave the room. As soon as the teacher was gone, Suzanne jumped up. "They're all around us! They're all around us!" she cried out. She looked really scared.

Mandy leaped up. *"Aaaahhh!"* she screamed. "They're all around us!"

George stared at the girls. "What's going on?" he asked nervously.

"Look! They're all around us!" Suzanne cried out again.

"Oh, no!" Kevin said as he looked under the table

"Look everywhere. They're all around us!" Zoe added.

Manny started to cry.

Jeremy pulled his legs up onto his chair. "*What's* all around us?" he asked nervously.

Suzanne stopped screaming. "The walls. *The walls* are all around us!" She laughed so hard she couldn't stop.

"You big scaredy-cats," Miriam teased. "You should have seen your faces."

Katie looked at the boys. Their faces weren't scared anymore. They were angry.

"That was a great one, huh, Katie?" Suzanne asked her best friend.

Katie nodded. "You really got them," she said. "But I wonder what they're going to do to get us back."

Chapter 10

That afternoon, Katie walked home from
school by herself. Her mom was waiting for
her on the front porch.

"Where's Jeremy?" Katie's mom asked as
Katie walked up the stairs to the house.

Katie shrugged. "I have no idea."

Katie's mom seemed surprised. "I thought
Wednesday was your special day with Jeremy.
You two *always* spend Wednesday afternoons
together."

It was true. Most of the other kids had
activities on Wednesday afternoons. Suzanne
took ballet classes. George and Kevin had
tae kwon do. Manny had his piano lessons.

But Katie and Jeremy were always free on Wednesdays. That was their playdate day.

"Jeremy doesn't play with girls anymore," Katie said sadly.

"Oh, I see," Katie's mom said.

"It really stinks!" Katie exclaimed.

"I agree," her mother said. "Maybe he'll change his mind."

Katie shook her head. "I don't think so, Mom. I don't think any of the boys will ever talk to a girl again."

Katie's mom laughed. "Oh, they will. Don't you worry."

Katie sighed. She wished she could believe her mom.

"Do you want a snack?" Katie's mother asked.

Katie shook her head. "I don't feel much like eating."

"So, what do you want to do?"

"There's nothing to do," Katie told her. "I am so bored!"

"Do you have any homework?" her mother asked.

Katie rolled her eyes. How could her mother think about homework at a time like this?

Just then Pepper came running outside. He licked Katie's hand. Katie pet his head but didn't smile. Pepper tugged at Katie's pant leg with his teeth. Katie moved her leg away. Pepper looked up at Katie with his big, brown eyes. He let out a loud bark.

"I think he wants to go for a walk," Katie's mom said finally. "Why don't you take him? It's better than just sitting around here all afternoon."

"I guess," Katie agreed. "Come on, Pepper."

Pepper leaped up and ran eagerly down the block. Katie followed behind him. When they reached the end of Katie's street, Pepper turned right and kept walking. Before Katie realized where she was going, Pepper had led her to Jeremy's house.

Jeremy was out on the lawn playing soccer.

Well, not *playing*, actually. He was just sort of dribbling the ball back and forth. That's all you can do when you play soccer alone.

As soon as Pepper saw Jeremy, he raced onto the lawn. Pepper loved playing ball with Jeremy. The cocker spaniel barked excitedly. He used his brown-and-white snout to steal Jeremy's soccer ball and push it across the lawn.

"Hey, cut that out!" Jeremy shouted at the dog.

"Don't you yell at my dog," Katie told Jeremy.

"Then get your dog away from my ball," Jeremy told her. "He's ruining my practice."

"Oh, big deal," Katie argued back. "He's just having fun."

"Well, let him have fun somewhere else. Take him over to one of your *girlfriends'* houses," Jeremy said.

"I would if I could," Katie replied. "No one's home."

"What are you doing here anyway?" Jeremy asked. "Did you come to spy on me?"

Katie frowned. "You're not that interesting."

"Then why are you here?" Jeremy asked. "I was just following Pepper. *He* was the one who came over here. But don't worry, we're leaving."

Katie turned toward her dog. But he wasn't on the lawn. She looked around. Pepper wasn't there.

"He must be in the backyard," Jeremy said.

"You'd better get him before he walks all over my mom's flowers."

"Come on, Pepper," Katie called. But Pepper didn't come.

"Pepper! Here boy!" Katie shouted, louder this time. But the dog still didn't answer her call.

"Pepper!" Jeremy screamed. "Get out here!"

The kids waited a minute. When Pepper still didn't come running, Katie's heart began to pound.

"Oh, no!" she cried. "Pepper's gone!"

Chapter 11

"He probably just went home," Jeremy said. "He knows the way there."

"Maybe," Katie answered hopefully. "I'm going to go check right now." She ran off toward her house.

"Wait up!" Jeremy called after her. "I'll go with you."

They raced to Katie's house. Jeremy searched Katie's yard. Katie ran inside and looked in all the rooms. She wanted to tell her mom what had happened, but she was talking on the phone. So Katie looked under the beds and in the closets all by herself. But Pepper wasn't there.

"This is awful!" Katie cried when she met Jeremy outside. "Pepper's never just run off like this! What if he doesn't know how to get back?"

"That won't happen," Jeremy assured her. "Pepper knows this neighborhood really well. He'll find you."

"We have to keep looking," Katie said. "He's got to be around somewhere."

Jeremy and Katie spent the next hour looking for Pepper. They looked in their neighbors' yards. They peered under bushes

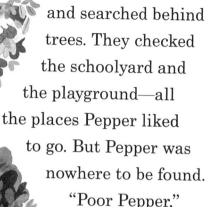

and searched behind trees. They checked the schoolyard and the playground—all the places Pepper liked to go. But Pepper was nowhere to be found.

"Poor Pepper," Katie cried. "He's lost and all alone. He's probably really scared. Oh, Jeremy! What if I never see him again?"

"Someone will find him," Jeremy told her. "He's got all those tags on him. Whoever finds him is sure to call you."

"I have to make signs!" Katie said. "I'll offer a reward for him."

"Come on. Let's go to my house and make some signs," Jeremy suggested.

Katie followed Jeremy home.

"You go sit on the deck in the backyard." Jeremy said. "I'll get paper and markers."

Katie did as she was told. She flopped down in one of the plastic chairs on the deck. She began to sob.

"Oh, *Pepper*! I miss you so much," she cried.

Just then Katie heard a little bark.

"Pepper?" she called out.

There was another little bark. Then Pepper came bounding out from underneath Jeremy's backyard deck. He had an old, soggy tennis ball in his mouth.

Katie sobbed even harder. But this time she was crying tears of joy. She hugged her dog tightly and kissed his little, round head. "Pepper! You're okay!"

Jeremy came out of the house carrying a pile of construction paper and some markers.

"Jeremy, look who's here," Katie exclaimed.

"Pepper! Boy, were we worried about you," Jeremy stroked one of Pepper's long, furry ears. "Where was he?"

"Under the deck, I think. We didn't look there. He might have been there the whole time."

"Why would he go under the deck?"

Katie frowned. "He probably hid there because he couldn't stand us fighting," she said. "He hates when people yell."

"I guess we *were* pretty loud," Jeremy admitted. Then he stopped for a minute and smiled at Katie. "You know, I forgot we weren't supposed to be talking to each other."

"Me, too," Katie said. "I'm really sorry. I mean about Suzanne's party and everything."

"I'm sorry about the Boys Club. It was a dumb idea," Jeremy apologized.

"So, are we friends again?" Katie asked.

Jeremy smiled. "We were always friends," he said.

Katie sighed. "You know, you don't have to talk to me at school or anything if you don't want to. The boys don't have to know we're still best friends."

"That's dumb," Jeremy said. "We can be friends with whoever we want."

"Yeah," Katie agreed.

"The only problem is, everyone else is going to be mad at us for being friends," Jeremy said sadly.

Katie thought about that. Then suddenly she got one of her great ideas. "I know a way we can stop that from happening!" she said excitedly. She grabbed a piece of paper and a magic marker. "Here's what we do . . ."

Chapter 12

Manny, Kevin, and George sure were surprised when they got to school Thursday morning. They found Jeremy sitting under a tree . . . with *Katie*!

"Jeremy!" Kevin exclaimed. "What are you doing with her?"

"I hope you brought along a lot of cootie spray," George added. "She's loaded with them!"

"Cut it out George," Jeremy said. "Katie's my friend. She's your friend, too—in case you forgot."

George covered his ears. "Stop talking like that! That's not how members of the Boys

Club should sound."

"I'm not in the Boys Club anymore," Jeremy told him.

"Why not?" Kevin asked.

Before Jeremy could answer, Suzanne, Miriam, Mandy, and Zoe walked over to the tree.

"Come on, Katie," Suzanne said. "We have a Girls Club meeting now."

Katie shook her head. "I'm not in the Girls Club anymore."

"What?" Suzanne asked with surprise.

"Jeremy and I are starting a new club," Katie explained. "The BUG Club." She held up a picture she'd drawn. It was a picture of a ladybug and a bumblebee.

"The BUG club," George laughed. "That's perfect for girls. The *cootie* bug club!"

"Not funny," Jeremy said. "BUG stands for Boys United with Girls."

"Isn't that BUWG?" Mandy asked.

"I know," Katie admitted. "But that doesn't

spell anything. So we're just calling it the BUG Club."

"I think the BUG Club sounds awful," Suzanne said.

"It's a great club," Jeremy told her. "We're going to do all kinds of fun things."

"And we're not going to fight like your clubs do," Katie added.

"What kind of things are you going to do?" Manny asked.

"Well, for starters, we're going ice skating at Skyrink this weekend," Katie said.

"This weekend?" Suzanne asked. "But my party is this weekend."

"And we were going to go to the amusement park," Manny reminded Jeremy.

"But that's on Saturday," Katie said. "The BUG Club is going skating on Sunday."

"That way we can do everything," Jeremy added.

"It's okay to do things just with girls or boys *sometimes*," Katie said. "But that doesn't mean we can't all hang out together other times."

"That's what the BUG Club is all about," Jeremy explained. "Everybody being friends."

"Well, ice skating *is* fun," Kevin said.

"I do have this adorable purple skating dress," Suzanne thought out loud. "It's got glitter on the skirt."

"The BUG Club, huh?" Zoe said. "That sounds kind of cute."

Katie looked over at Jeremy and smiled. The first meeting of the BUG Club was working out just fine.

Chapter 13

Katie laughed as she saw George holding onto the side of the rink. He was trying not to fall. He'd never been ice skating before. "Come on George, you can do it!" Katie cheered him on.

George tried to smile. "You know what the hardest part of skating is, Katie Kazoo?" he joked.

"No. What?"

"The ice!" George answered. He rubbed his rear end. George had done a lot of falling today.

Katie giggled. "You're getting better," she assured him.

Suzanne skated up to Katie. "This BUG Club is a lot of fun," she said. "I just wish I wasn't so sleepy."

"You're the one who wanted to stay up all night," Katie reminded her. "The rest of us fell asleep before the movie was over."

Suzanne gave her a tired smile. "I told you. Nobody is supposed to sleep at a sleepover."

Just then, Jeremy shouted across the ice. "Hey everyone, let's do the BUG Club cheer!"

"Yeah!" The kids cried out.

"Buzz, buzz, buzz! Zap, zap, sting! If you're in the BUG Club, friends are everything!"

As Katie listened to her friends cheer, she felt a cool breeze hit the back of her neck. Oh no! Was this magic wind again? Who was she going to turn into now?

Then Katie remembered that she was at an ice-skating rink. The whole room was breezy. She was *supposed* to feel cold.

Katie wrapped her scarf a little tighter around her neck and skated around the rink with her friends. She didn't want to think about the magic wind. She was happy just being Katie.

At least for now.

Jeremy's Soccer Center

If you play soccer or if you want to learn how, this chapter's for you. It's filled with tips from Jeremy Fox—the best soccer player in class 3A.

1. Always warm up before you play. If you don't, you might hurt your muscles. If you're playing on a cold day, do your warm-ups in a sweatsuit to keep your muscles warm. Don't take the sweatsuit off until game time.

2. Don't use your hands (unless you're the goalie).

3. When you're trying to score a goal, where you kick the ball is more important than how hard you kick it. A well-placed shot is more likely to go into the goal.

4. Never turn your back on the ball. Keep your eyes on the ball at all times!

5. If you are a defensive player, it's your job to stay between the ball and the goal whenever you can.

6. If you are a forward, switch positions with the other forwards on your team. For instance, have the left wing switch places with the center. It's a good way to confuse the other team.

7. Always talk to your teammates when you are on the field. Let them know if the ball is coming their way or if someone is sneaking up beside them.

8. If you are a defensive player who is trapped, pass the ball to your goalkeeper for safety. Just make sure your goalie is ready for the pass. You don't want to kick the ball past him and into your own goal.

9. Don't dribble the ball on your own when you can make a safe pass to another player.

10. Always respect the referee's decision. Being a good sport is part of being a great player.

About the Author

Nancy Krulik is the author of more than 150 books for children and young adults, including three *New York Times* best sellers. She lives in New York City with her husband, composer Daniel Burwasser, and their children, Amanda and Ian. When she's not busy writing the Katie Kazoo, Switcheroo series, Nancy loves swimming, reading, and going to the movies.

About the Illustrators

John & Wendy have illustrated all of the Katie Kazoo books, but when they're not busy drawing Katie and her friends, they like to paint, take photographs, travel, and play music in their rock 'n' roll band. They live and work in Brooklyn, New York.

Katie Kazoo
SWITCHEROO

Read all the books in the
KATIE KAZOO,
SWITCHEROO series!